T0207681

Night in the Galaxies

Night in the Galaxies

AN OBSERVATION OF LIFE

ROCK DiLISIO

NIGHT IN THE GALAXIES
AN OBSERVATION OF LIFE

Copyright © 2016 Rock DiLisio.

Editors:
Erica M. Hollabaugh
Brianna L. Flasco

All rights reserved. No part of this book may be used or reproduced by any means, graphic, electronic, or mechanical, including photocopying, recording, taping or by any information storage retrieval system without the written permission of the author except in the case of brief quotations embodied in critical articles and reviews.

This is story of fiction. All characters, names, incidents, organizations, and dialogue in this novel are either products of the author's imagination or are used fictitiously.

Developed in the UCLA Feature Film Screenplay Program.

iUniverse books may be ordered through booksellers or by contacting:

iUniverse
1663 Liberty Drive
Bloomington, IN 47403
www.iuniverse.com
1-800-Authors (1-800-288-4677)

Because of the dynamic nature of the Internet, any web addresses or links contained in this book may have changed since publication and may no longer be valid. The views expressed in this work are solely those of the author and do not necessarily reflect the views of the publisher, and the publisher hereby disclaims any responsibility for them.

Any people depicted in stock imagery provided by Thinkstock are models, and such images are being used for illustrative purposes only. Certain stock imagery © Thinkstock.

ISBN: 978-1-5320-0913-6 (sc)
ISBN: 978-1-5320-0914-3 (e)

Print information available on the last page.

iUniverse rev. date: 11/01/2016

CHAPTER 1

July 7, 1947 – Roswell, New Mexico – Reported crash of an Unidentified Flying Object (UFO)

The U.S. military has altered the reports of what actually occurred on that date four times since 1947. The first, unfiltered military report was clear and accurate. On July 8, 1947, Army-Air Force Public Information Officer, Lieutenant Walter Haut, released the following approved statement:

"The Army Air Force has recovered the wreckage of a crashed disk."

The long nights of scanning the heavens have, at times, been monotonous. This is especially the case when you pull a solo shift. That shift is one where you end up talking to the stars, which also happens to be a very effective response when someone asks my line of work. Many times they think I'm a Hollywood reporter, which I casually shrug off, since those stars get their namesake after mine.

Tonight is special, though, and I have several members of the star searchers with me on this shift. Yes, it's comet watch night and we're looking for a fiery one to come by. Everyone is in position at his or her respective station, one that slightly resembles the bridge on the Starship Enterprise from *Star Trek*. Remember, it's a star ship…not a space ship… big difference.

Heads down and determined everyone was working hard at lining up control points. Levers were smoothly slid across grids and digital dials bounced across various screens providing a warm glow to an otherwise darkened room. The enormous refractor telescope rose from the darkness like a giant awakening from slumber. Our crew rotated the scope's bulk sideways and upward and positioned it for the ultimate observation point.

High above our heads, the dome slowly, methodically slid open to the beckoning sky. I rotated it into position, via known coordinates provided by other observatories across the world that had already recorded their observation. Reports have flowed in stating that the comet is large, fiery and in the projected orbit. We have a short wait and the intensity in the room builds.

Across the large screen comes an update that the comet's coordinates are being adjusted and the new figures soon appear. I move from my observation position at the telescope and back to my station to adjust the dome's viewing angle. I inserted the new coordinates in a routine fashion, only to see no movement by the dome. I insert the information again and there is still no movement. As they continue their work, worried looks begin to appear on the faces of the astronomer's. They had the hottest ticket in town and may now be late for the show.

I requested that the dome move once more…nothing…and again, no reaction. No words passed between the scientists, they kept their heads down and continued with their respective tasks. Words were not necessary, they knew what had to be done and I jumped into action. Reaching the nearest ladder, I quickly climbed towards the cavernous dome for a manual override. The higher I climbed, the more I could feel the cool night air as it poured through the opening.

Reaching the catwalk, I could see the large screen projecting the comet to pass above us in three minutes. I sprinted to my destination and worked feverishly at the controls that locked the manual lever. I peeked over the railing again and saw the countdown at 30 seconds. The lever now unlocked, I laid my weight into it in an attempt to move it more quickly.

The dome shuttered and I rotated the gears quickly, but with great effort. Inch-by-inch it moved to its right. Luckily, inches were all that was needed. There was not enough time for me to return to my station, so I peered through the dome. Far in the distance a streak of fire smoothly and succinctly flew across the black sky. Applause rose from the bridge of the Enterprise…a star was born.

In comparison to the night before, the following night was semi-anticlimactic as you can imagine. The data and most of the analysis of the comet's passing was handled by the day light staff, leaving only a few clean-up operations for the 'night-shift,' which comprised of Cal Norcross and his colleague, Jess Braxton.

The excitement of the remaining comet work kept them enthralled in the first few hours, but work soon returned to their normal routine, which was the nightly search for specific stars and measuring the distances between them. The observatory also delved into the quest of finding another earth-like planet and the excitement of discovering such kept the astronomers keenly locked into their tasks. Cal and Jess sat next to each other in front of their control panels and large screen computer terminals. Their seats also had easy access to the enormous refractor telescope that peered nightly into the heavens.

Cal initiated his photometry programs and casually looked to his right to gain the attention of his attractive young, blonde co-worker. 'Did we get a dimensions reading on the comet? That's our expertise and I'm sure they'll be looking for it in the morning.'
'Should have that info soon, Cal. Still running it through the system.' Jess replied with only a slight glance in the direction of her dark-haired, athletically built colleague.
Cal nodded and continued working a dial on the control panel. 'You know that Boss Hog is going to want that on his desk first thing. If we get anything done tonight it should be that.'
Jess snickered. 'Professor *Hogan* will have his data…no worries. I'm just running it through again to make sure the calculations are correct, but the system is slow tonight. We can at least give them preliminary calculations by morning.'
Cal picks up a piece of paper on his desk and reads it under a desk light. 'This memo states that the newspapers will be here in the A.M. They will be interviewing the Hog-meister about the comet.'
Jess laughed loudly.
'Quiet!' Cal replied with a calming hand motion. 'You know that sound carries at night. They can hear you through the dome.' He smiled.

Jess covered her mouth, but continued her laughter. 'Stop it with that… the professor is not all that bad.'

Cal laughed. 'I know, but you also know how he gets when something of high-profile is going on.'

'Speaking of high-profile,' Jess said without stopping her work. 'You were pretty impressive last night…you know, with the manual override of the dome.'

Cal stopped his work for a moment and glanced quickly at Jess. 'Thanks. It was my shift, so I was the one who should handle that. No big deal.'

Jess smiled without looking at him. 'Yeah, I know, but you can move a lot faster then I thought.'

'Hey…I'm an athletic type…shouldn't surprise you too much.' Cal said with another quick look.

'I see that…' She replied with a sly smile.

'While we're thinking about it,' He answered. 'Let's run a diagnostic on the system to see what the malfunction was with the dome…don't want that to happen again.'

'Absolutely…let's get the comet data back first and we'll get right on it.' Jess said and then laughs. She begins to sway in her chair to some unheard melody.

Cal glances at her with a perplexed look on his face. 'What the hell… are you doing?'

Jess breaks directly into song. '*Get right on it….Get right on it…*' She continues with her swaying in an even more accentuated manner.

Cal shakes his head and smiles. 'You know…not bad…but, save your singing practice for after work.'

'I sometimes practice in here before the next shift arrives…great acoustics. Did you know that?' She glances quickly at Cal and then to her computer screen.

'I've heard rumors.' He replies wryly. 'You're still trying to make a go of it…your singing career, I mean?'

'Sure, why not?' She says without turning. 'I could use the extra cash if something comes of it…a young, university astronomer can only make so much, you know. I even have a recording session to make a demo soon.'

'Hey, great! Glad to hear that it's progressing.' He turns and smiles at her. 'I've never heard you sing, but I wouldn't mind. What about a few bars of '*Get right on it*' right now?'

'I'm working…please.' She chuckles. 'I'll let the anticipation build.'

Cal shakes his head. 'Jess, someday…with your talent as an astronomer, you won't need a side job.'

'Thanks. Maybe, but I want something to fall back on. Even so, I'm not a former NASA recruit like you and certainly not as driven in this field. I'm not looking to have a star named after me like you are.'

'A galaxy preferable, but I'll settle for a star.' He laughs. Even though Cal was one of NASA's best, young talents, he left to pursue a teaching opportunity at the university, which he performed twice a week in early afternoon classes. NASA, however, still maintains his phone number on speed dial and uses it frequently in an attempt to lure him back.

She looks directly at him. 'Heck, you even want to win the Nobel Prize…I just want a promotion to pay off some bills.'

Just then, the intern arrives with the data on the comet.

'Here are the new data reports that you asked for.' She hands them to Cal.

'Thanks, Courtney.' Cal says to the smallish brunette with her hair tightly wrapped in a bun. She smiles and leaves.

'See,' Jess says. 'I told you that the professor would have his information.'

'Keeps me from getting Hog-tied too.' Cal breaks into laughter.

CHAPTER 2

In 1972 and 1973, NASA launched the spacecrafts Pioneer 10 and Pioneer 11, respectively. Each carried a pair of gold-anodized aluminum plaques that provided information about Earth. The anticipation is that the spacecraft will be intercepted by extraterrestrial life.

The following day, Cal is torn from his mid-morning slumber by a call from the observatory's administrative assistant. The local newspapers had interviewed Professor Hogan and he mentioned how resourceful his staff was, especially in light of the dome malfunction. The reporters had asked for the reason of the malfunction, which Professor Hogan couldn't answer appropriately. He promised them a reply by the afternoon; hence, the urgent call to Cal.

Cal explained that the diagnostics on the hemispherical dome malfunction were just completed by the end of his shift and he didn't have time to send a report to university officials, nor did he have an opportunity to provide a thorough analysis of the report, which he barely looked at. He sits in a chair in his bedroom and immediately sends a text to Jess asking her if she reviewed the report before she left. She replies that she had not had a chance and expected to review it when she returned to work that night. Cal explained the situation and asked if she could meet him at the coffee shop within the hour, where they would access the report together. She agrees and Cal quickly heads for the shower.

At the expected time, Cal enters the brown-walled coffee shop and spots Jess seated in the rear and already working her laptop and a cup of coffee. He walks up to the table and bumps it. Jess looks up in an annoyed fashion.

'Hey girl, you look pretty good for someone just roused from a deep slumber.'

She cracks a slight smile. 'Thanks…you don't.' The smile widens.

'They know better than to mess with my sleep…shouldn't they?' He says as he takes the other chair at the table. He waves to get the waitress' attention.

'By the time that your coffee arrives,' Jess says as she busily types at the computer keys. 'I'll have the dome info for you. The preliminary reports show it to be a programming error. Didn't maintenance perform a mechanical review a few weeks ago?'

Cal scratches his chin as his coffee arrives. 'Yes, they did. They were still working on it when I showed up that day.' He pauses. 'You know that Wilcox deactivates the program when maintenance is performed?'

Jess' eyes widen. 'That's right! It's a safety precaution.'

'Wilcox always plays with the program while they're doing the maintenance.' Cal replies between sips. 'He keeps trying to speed up the dome's open and closure times. I bet he added or deleted something in the programming that caused the issue.'

'I agree.' Jess says as she stares intently at her screen. 'Here's the final report…it does confirm a programming error, which deters the dome from opening at certain times of the day. This is solid enough to send.'

'Send it…the professor will be happy to get it so soon.' Cal says as he sits back in his chair. 'Up for a walk…after coffee?'

'Sure, why not? It's a beautiful day and I need to stop at the pharmacy to pick up some eye drops.' She replies as she emphatically sends off the email to Professor Hogan.

The neighborhoods in this portion of the city were some of the best and the main street was equally as quaint. The well-kept buildings and manicured landscapes made this mid-city neighborhood feel as though you were in small town America. They strolled the streets on what was developing into a beautiful fall day.

Cal points to the antique store up ahead. 'I need to stop in there…I was going to come this afternoon, but I'm here now.'

'What's the big interest with the antique store?' Jess asks as she walks casually with her hands in her pockets.

'I thought that you liked antiques?' Cal answers with a quick glance towards her.

'I do…didn't know that you did.' She returns the glance.

'I was getting a coffee the other day and just sort of strolled in there on the way home. I saw something in there…not sure that they know what it is.' He stares at the approaching small storefront.

'And? What was it?' Jess asks.

'A moon rock. A very unusual one too.' He replies.

'A moon rock!' Jess replies excitedly and stops in her tracks under a tree. 'They have a moon rock in there?'

Cal had also stopped under the same tree. 'I'm certain of it. They said it was a piece of anthracite but, I'm sure that they're mistaken.'

'Why didn't you buy it? I'm sure that you know what they're worth and those shouldn't be in private hands. The university would have reimbursed you…they'd love to have it.' Jess said.

'I know that, but it was in the thousands and I didn't have that much in my checking account at the time.' Cal shook his head and brushed back his hair. 'He doesn't accept credit, so I told him I'd be back this week.'

'Wow…that's great…let's go and take a look.' Jess replied as she again began to stroll.

Entering the store they immediately noticed the shop owner, a graying, middle-aged, affluently dressed man, lifting a heavy marble horse from a display table and carrying it to the backroom. He lumbers under its weight, but a smile seemingly crosses his face as he thinks of the sale of the highly collectible horse. Hearing the door chime he finds his way past the curtain that separates the storage room and the store and back into view.

'Good morning, may I help you?' He asks as Cal and Jess walk towards the counter.

'Mr. Painter,' Cal said. 'I was here the other day and was interested in your unusual rock.' Cal looks around the room for it as he approaches.

'Yes, I remember you. Unfortunately, that item is in the process of being sold. Today actually.' Mr. Painter replies with a shrug.

Cal is slightly startled and braces himself on the counter. 'Really? Has it been sold or hasn't it been?'

'Well, technically not, someone will be here within the half-hour and their intent is to purchase it.' The shop owner replies.

'Mr. Painter, I'm interested in purchasing it and I'm here now. What more can you ask? The other party may not even show.' Cal answers knowing emphatically that he can't let the rock get into private hands.

Mr. Painter nods slowly. 'Sir, I apologize, but I have promised to hold the rock for them and I believe that they will be interested enough to show up as expected.'

'I see, but still, would you consider an offer?' Cal asks. 'You see, I'm a curator of sorts with these rocks and this piece is one that I would really like to add to the collection. Your price was $5,000.00...I'm sure your buyer is paying full or less-than-full price. What do you say to $5,500?' Cal makes direct eye contact.

'Very generous of you, but I must keep my promise to the other buyer who agreed to my price yesterday.' Mr. Painter answers shuffling the papers in front of him for no particular reason. 'I know that you were interested in it the other day, but you didn't purchase it and I didn't know if you would return.'

'$6,000. I'm very, very interested, Mr. Painter. Then again, maybe the other buyer would like to make a quick profit.' Cal replies with a slight smile.

'I do not want the other buyer pressured, Sir. Again, I must keep my word. Please understand that I have a business reputation to keep. May

I suggest that you have a cup of coffee at the cafe across the street and maybe return in an hour? I will fill you in on the situation and whether the rock did sell.' Painter stumbles over his words. He is flustered and stuffs the papers into a folder. 'If it doesn't sell, we can discuss it.'

'Maybe I should be honest with you.' Cal stated as he turned to a nearby table. He admires a few objects, slightly touching them. He picks one up and holds it close to his face. 'Do you know what that rock really is?'

'Of course,' Mr. Painter answers while breaking out a handkerchief from his coat pocket and wipes his brow.

Cal moves towards the counter and pulls a card case from his jacket. He hands Mr. Painter his card showing that he is a university astronomer.

'Pleased to have you in my store, Mr. Norcross.' The shop owner replies. 'I read about in you in the press...you worked at NASA, correct? You were in the astronaut program too?'

Cal nods. 'Yes, and that is why I have an interest in the rock. I now hope that you understand my sincere interest and why I would like to purchase it.' With a slight smile, he again leans on the counter and looks directly at Painter.

Mr. Painter shrugs. 'Not really, is there something specific about this rock then? Even so, I sympathize with you, but I cannot go back on my promise to the other party. My hands are tied.' Painter nervously begins to tap the card on the counter. The ticking clock in the corner of the shop sounds like an engine to him.

'There is.' Cal replies. 'If you won't sell it to me...we may have to approach the party that is buying it.'

Painter mops his brow again. 'Mr. Norcross, the person who is buying it is highly influential and will not resell the rock. He is an avid collector and will not take kindly to you approaching him about the subject. I do not want a scene in my shop. Please, go to the cafe and stop back later.'

'Then what?' Jess finally chimes in.

'If they don't purchase it...the problem has been resolved. If they do, then I will mention your visit and give them your card.' Painter answers. 'If he wants to contact you...he can.'

'There is no guarantee in that scenario.' Cal states. 'That rock is special and the university would like to have it.'

The antique ticking clock now sounds like a time bomb for Painter. The sound disappears as an even more frightening sound is heard...the chime of the door.

'Mr. Wellson...' Mr. Painter said sheepishly. 'It appears that this gentleman would like to speak to you before we make the transaction for the rock.' Painter wringed his hands nervously and then quickly ushered him in Cal's direction.

'What's the meaning of this?' Wellson asked as he walked towards Cal. The look on his face was stoic and he appeared unamused.

Cal stood with his arms crossed and looked Wellson directly in the eye as he approached. Jess took a few steps back.

'Mr. Wellson, is it?' Cal offered a handshake, which was briefly returned.

'Excuse me, Sir, but I understand that you are interested in a rock from Mr. Painter?'

'I have agreed to purchase it and I'm here to finalize the deal.' He replied defiantly.

'Are you aware of what you are purchasing?' Cal asked.

'Of course!' Wellson snorted. 'It's anthracite.'

Cal smiled. 'I wouldn't be so certain of that.'

'What are you saying, young man? I'm an avid collector.'

'Sir, I'm an astronomer at the university, as is my colleague here.' He said pointing to Jess.

'And.....' Wellson replied irritated.

'And...that is not anthracite. That, Mr. Wellson, is a moon rock.'

Wellson stood silently. He appeared to ponder the suggestion and a slight smile crossed his face. 'Maybe you are correct. Even so, a moon rock would be a great addition to my collection.'

Cal sighed and once again crossed his arms. 'I'm sure that it would... except that they are illegal to sell.'

Mr. Painter moaned and pulled out his handkerchief to wipe his brow. 'What do you mean?' Wellson asked.

Jess moved into the conversation. 'Per United States law, moon rocks are considered National Treasures and cannot be sold.'

Mr. Painter moved from behind the counter and pulled Wellson to the side for a personal conversation.

Jess leaned towards Cal. 'We can't let him walk out of here with that rock. I actually think that he knew what it was all along.'

'I know...but, I think the legality of the transaction may change the situation.' Cal replied as he watched the two men speaking.

Mr. Painter left Wellson's side and walked hesitantly towards the astronomers. He brushed the clump of hair atop his head with his hand. 'Could I possibly have a friend of mine...a geologist...take a look at the rock to confirm what it is? He's here in town and could possibly be here within the hour.'

'Sure,' Cal answered. 'That'll be fine, but I'm certain that it's a moon rock.'

Painter nodded and grinned. 'It may be, but I'd like to know for sure.'

'That'll be fine, Mr. Painter.' Jess replied. 'I have to stop at a few places, so we can do that now and come back later.'

Cal and Jess returned to find that Mr. Wellson had left the shop without purchasing the moon rock. We didn't ask questions and accepted our good fortune. Mr. Painter stated that we were free to purchase the rock if we could ensure that it was going to the university. Obviously, Mr. Painter had quickly moved to a state of self-preservation. We agreed and offered to have him visit us and view the rock when it goes on display. With that, the transaction was done.

Later that day, after Cal had instructed his afternoon astronomy class at the university, he and Jess decided to show up for work early in order to present the rock to Dr. Hogan. He was ecstatic about the specimen and immediately contacted the university finance department to arrange for Cal's reimbursement. Since they had "found" the rock, he also stated that Cal and Jess would be primarily responsible to research it and that process could begin immediately this week. The Professor also stated that he would have to contact NASA and inform them that we had it in our possession. Cal suggested that he be on the call also and that he would also assist in any related paperwork.

CHAPTER 3

In 1977, NASA launched the spacecrafts Voyager 1 and Voyager 2. Each contained a gold-plated copper disk containing sounds and images of Earth. The purpose was to communicate the story of our world to extraterrestrials.

Cal opened the observation dome as his shift began and found that the night was clear and crisp. A flash of cool air penetrated the observation room, but it was actually refreshing. Jess sat quietly to his right and worked the computer keyboard like a piano. Then again, she knew how to play and was musically inclined.

'When's the studio session?' Cal asked. 'You asked me if I'd like to come hear you sing.'

She turned quickly and smiled. 'You really want to go?'

'Sure…never been to a studio session before…it may be fun.'

She cleared her throat. 'Well then, it's actually tomorrow.'

'Tomorrow??' He caught himself before a shocked impression hit his face.

'Yes, can you make it?' She asked as she returned to her work.

'Yeah, yeah…I can make it.' Cal nodded heavily in his reply.

'Okay, great.' Jess replied seemingly pleased. '1:00 at FCI Studio, which is just a couple of blocks from here.'

Cal nodded and grinned. 'I know where it is. I'll be there…just make it good.'

The following day, Cal made good on his promise and went to the recording studio. He greeted Jess in the Green Room and wished her luck with a big hug and a little too close of an embrace. Jess appeared a little nervous, but not as much as Cal had expected. He began to think that maybe Jess had the confidence and talent to make something of this side career. He grabbed a cup of coffee that she offered from the studio freebies and headed towards a location where he was told he could see and hear the recording. On his way, he ran into a middle-aged gentleman who walked quickly towards the nearby recording booth. Cal asked if it was fine for him to watch from his given location and soon he discovered that he was speaking to Jess' 'agent,' Bill Watson, who graciously invited Cal to join him in the recording booth.

Bill Watson placed headphones on, but appeared uncomfortable in his chair as he watched the set-up occurring from behind the studio glass. He also took several gulps of his coffee, which he appeared to regard as his energy drink. Seated to his left, sat a very young, male studio technician who was slowly sliding controls back and forth on a panel. The amount of equipment in this room almost reminded Cal of his control panel at the observatory. Jess sat comfortably by her microphone on the other side of the glass wearing a white, airy dress and adjusted her headphones as she waited for her cue. Noticing Cal in the booth, she smiled widely and waved.

'Okay, Jess, let's make it a good take this time. Last verse only,' Bill Watson said as he pushed the microphone button to speak to Jess. He takes another sip of coffee in what appears an attempt to wake up.

'Gotcha. I'm up for it.' Jess replied with a nod.

'Whenever you're ready...go for it.' Bill said.

Music began to fill the studio and Jess moved closer to the microphone. She swayed and then began to sing. "Time to fly...time to fly...you and I both know why..." Her eyes closed and she breaks into the verse and sings it through, while slowly swaying to the music.

Bill sips his coffee and rubs his forehead. As the verse concludes, he breathes deeply and sighs. The technician winces and rubs his eyes.

'Okay...okay...not bad.' Bill says hesitantly as he presses and releases the microphone button when he speaks to her.

'Not bad? I thought it was my best yet!' She replies with concern. Jess removes her headphones and stares at Bill through the glass.

'Let's take a break, huh? I need to make some sound adjustments in here. We'll regroup and start in about 15 minutes.' Bill answers as he removes his headphones and wipes his brow with a napkin.

The technician leans over to speak to him. They can't be heard from within the booth.

'Hey, man, she can't sing. Looks good...but, she can't sing. Just sayin...' He states emphatically to Bill and moves back to the control panel. Bill sheepishly looks over to Cal and smiles.

'Bill, I need to keep going...I'm in the groove. I'm starting to think that you're not into this.' Jess says from behind the glass.

'You're great, Jess. It's going to take time, that's all.' He replies and leans back in his chair.

'You promised that we'll get the song recorded today, so that we can get it to the music producer tomorrow.' She answers with concern.

The technician slowly looks towards Bill with a questioning glance.

'Well, it's not good enough yet. We'll get it there. It's big time for you, Jess...I promise, just be patient.' He replies with consternation.

'Thanks for the support, Bill. I know I'm almost there. My mom is really going to pump some money into your agency because you're helping my career.' Jess answers with a smile as she seats herself at a corner table and opens a bottle of water. Cal knew that Jess' family owned several auto dealerships and were somewhat known to be philanthropists. They had made large donations to the university after Jess was hired.

'So that's it, man? Her old lady is funding you? This is a big risk for your reputation and you are even talking to a producer? I mean, this girl is calling every cat in the neighborhood with that voice.' The technician said with a smirk.

'I know...I know, but things have been tough and I can use the funding right now...today. The producer never called me back, but she doesn't know that. Let me handle this, huh?' Bill whispers loudly to the technician. He then turns to Cal and shrugs.

'I'll be in touch with the producer tomorrow, Jess...I'll tell him we're refining the song.' He says to her after opening the microphone.

'I sure hope so; I'm only giving him one shot to sign me. This is your big ticket too, Bill. My mom also invests in other agencies, but I told her that I liked working with you.' Jess replies between sips of water. Cal was really impressed by her confidence, but after hearing her sing, wasn't certain that the talent was visible.

Bill rubs his eyes and gathers himself before he replies. 'It's my pleasure, Jess. I appreciate that your mother allows me to work with someone with your talent. We'll get this song down and keep moving forward.' He says with a slow nod.

'My man, you let her sing again and I'm going for the sound-deafening headphones.' The technician says.

'I can't wait to cut my CD.' Jess replies. 'Just a thought, do you have any ideas of how my music video should be done? I'm thinking an outdoor scene?'

'Just what I was thinking...yes, I have some ideas and I even have a producer lined up for that. We'll talk to him in a few weeks...yeah, in a few weeks.' Bill answers without hesitation and flings himself back into his chair. Cal began to squirm uncomfortably in his chair also.

'I'm so excited. I'm calling my mom right now and tell her.' She picks up her purse and digs through it.

'Outdoor music video? Better have a lot of kitty litter ready...' The technician chuckles.

'I don't have a video lined up...are you kidding? My six-year old sings Barney tunes better than she sings that song.' Bill replies looking intently at him.

'Now you're talking, guy. I wasn't coming out there to get arrested for noise pollution.' He shakes his head.

'My mom says that she wants to be in the video too. She also said that if things continue to progress, she will cut you the funding soon...oh, this is so great!' Jess says with excitement. Cal was seeing another side of Jess. At work she was more buttoned-up and reserved, but she's showing a lighter side to her personality and he liked it. Her singing talent was another subject.

Bill Watson clears his throat and hesitates before speaking. 'Did I tell you that I'm talking with the *Tonight Show* to have you on as a guest in the next six months...or so?' Bill surprisingly replied. Cal shot him an uncontrollable questioning glance and the technician dropped his head into his hands.

'Really?' Jess says staring through the glass. 'Wow, that's incredible! Let's get in more practice then.'

Bill nods and soon gives the go ahead for the recording to begin. Once again, Jess sways to the music and breaks into verse. On the desk, Bill and Cal's coffee cups steam in unison, almost matching the steam coming from the ears of the technician.

CHAPTER 4

———⟨∞⟩———

The Arecibo Observatory in Puerto Rico, fully completed in 2011, contains the largest radio telescope on Earth. Its primary purpose was to transmit a message about Earth to a global star cluster known as M13. It scans for transmissions or responses – 24/7. In September 2016, China completed an even larger radio telescope with the intention of discerning extraterrestrial signals.

Cal opened the hemispherical dome with his usual flair of pointing to the ceiling as it opened. He did little without theatrics, mostly to garner attention or a laugh. Jess, used to the routine, didn't even notice. He looked towards her in hopes of a reaction. His gaze made her glance in his direction.

'What?' She said shrugging her shoulders.

He shook his head. 'You're really into your work tonight.'

'No more than normal…just need to prep for the scan tonight.' She kept her head down and slowly slid several controls. 'Tonight, we're supposed to view the northern sector…back to extrasolar planet searches. We haven't done that in awhile.'

'Must be six-months…at least.' He replied. 'We've been too busy following up on the Hubble leads.'

'As fun as that was, we need to get back to a normal routine. Initiating the astrometry programs. Take me there, baby!' Jess said as she pointed to the dome.

Cal adjusted his seat and moved closer to his keyboard. Seconds later, the enormous refractor scope moved to its right in a slow, methodical fashion.

'Check your Sector 302, Jess. Mine is showing an anomaly.' Cal stated.

'Sector 302?' Jess asked as she moved to one of her screens.

'Something odd…' Cal replied as he worked his keyboard and scanned his screens.

'Wow…' Jess said slowly. 'What is that?'

'It's moving rapidly.' He said. 'Too high for a plane…not a meteorite either.'

'There's no trail…definitely not a meteorite.' Jess responded still staring at her screen.

'Ruling out a comet also.' Cal said. 'Initiating scope tracking. Let's get a few camera shots too.'

'Working on that now. Focusing the scope at high resolution.' Jess answered as her eyes moved from screen to screen.

'It's moving north to northeast. Stay with it, Jess.'

'Got it…increase the scope tracking speed…it's moving too fast.'

'Increase to Level 2…Wow!!' Cal said as he stood up. 'Did you see that!? Right angle turns on the dime!'

'Oh my!! I can't keep up with it. Increasing camera shutter speed…'

Cal returned to his seat. 'Increasing scope tracking speed to Level 3.'

'Pic 1…Pic 2…going for a third.' Jess replied. 'Not sure of the resolution, but we may have something.'

'Again confirming…for the record…this is not a plane or meteorite. Object is not within parameters, based on trajectory and atmospheric location.' Cal answered.

'That's for certain, Cal…just can't be. Increasing scope magnification.'

Cal worked quickly at his controls. 'Another turn! Now look! It stopped and is just sitting there.'

'You're right…it just stopped!' Jess exclaimed with her hands out in front of her in disbelief. 'I need to lock onto that position and increase magnification.'

'Better hurry, Jess…it's starting to move.'

'Locking! I need another few seconds…dam it! It's gone!' Jess replied.

'Moving north to northwest at a high rate of velocity.' Cal moved to another screen. 'Amazing! That was from a standstill position!'

'I have nothing…lost it.' Jess said as she frantically worked her controls.

'Confirmed…it's gone.' Cal said as he threw himself into his chair.

Jess leaned back into her chair also and sighed heavily. For several long and drawn-out moments, no words were spoken by either of them.

Jess finally turned towards Cal. 'What was that? I have nothing…'

Cal shrugged. 'Honestly, I'm not sure. I suppose it's what we think it is… it's *unidentified*. At least that's what my report will state.'

Jess sighed again. 'Yeah…I guess we'll have to write this up. It's not going to be easy.'

'I'll start the report now and you can finish it later.' Cal said. 'We should do our due diligence and contact the airport and the Air Force base to see if they can corroborate the sighting.'

Jess nodded. 'I'll do that tomorrow when we come in.'

'It will be interesting to hear what they know.' Cal replied rising from his chair. 'I need a drink, but I guess coffee will have to do. Want some?'

'Yes…please.' Cal stopped in his tracks and stared intently towards the corner of the large room. 'Jess…take a look. The moon rock…it's glowing!'

CHAPTER 5

On August 21, 2001, two crop circles appeared near the Chilbolton Observatory in Hampshire, England. Some astronomers interpreted the circles as an alien response to the Arecibo Observatory transmission from 1974.

The following day, Professor Hogan called Jess and Cal into work early. They immediately assumed it was due to their preliminary report they had submitted on the odd sighting the previous night. Both carried their first cup of evening coffee into the Professor's office. The middle-aged, well-dressed Professor was working at his white board, but he quickly moved to his desk when he heard the knock on his open oak door.

'Well, good to see that the night shift has reported to work.' He smiled slightly. 'Have a seat you two.' He waved them towards the chairs in front of his desk.

'Let me guess, Professor,' Cal began. 'You read the report from last night?' The Professor nodded and held the report up in front of him. 'Yes, I did.' He placed the report softly on his desk. 'Tell me…what's this all about?' Cal cleared his throat. 'The report stands on its own, Professor. We'll both verify what it states.'

Professor Hogan looked intently at the two of them. 'Are you implying what I think that you may be…implying?'

Jess placed her hand on Cal's arm and he took notice of the gesture. 'I'm very dedicated to my job, Professor.' She said confidently. 'Even though that report is only preliminary…I signed it, so I concur with the contents.' The Professor leaned back into his chair. He turned to his left and pointed at the white board. 'I made a schematic of the coordinates from your report.' He stood up and slowly walked towards the board.

'These calculations show an "object" moving at speeds five times greater than anything flying today. Beyond that, look at the trajectory…a fly couldn't change directions that quickly!' He began to connect the points depicted on the board to show the movement patterns.

'We checked the coordinates twice last night.' Cal said while viewing the board. 'If you check the scope's visual tracking patterns it reflects those results.'

Professor Hogan turned and looked at them. 'What you are suggesting is not possible.'

'Professor,' Jess said as she sat forward. 'I was able to take a few camera shots. I'm not sure they will turn out well, but they should show something.'

'That would be interesting to see, Jess.' He replied while replacing the cap on his marker.

Jess nodded. 'We'll also contact the airport and the Air Force base to see if they picked anything up.'

The Professor sighed and sat on the corner of his desk. 'Not sure how that will go over in the President's office. If you do so, I don't know about it.'

The two astronomers returned to their cubicles in the administrative section of the observatory. Both sat at their adjoining desks and worked their computers in what was a normal routine before the start of their shift.

Jess cleared her throat. 'I'm going to make a few phone calls now…maybe we'll get some confirmation.' She pulled her list of phone numbers from a drawer.

'Okay…I'll check on the photos.' Cal replied already moving from his seat. 'Galloway said he'd have them ready by this evening.'

Cal returned in minutes with a white envelope underneath his arm. He stood by Jess' desk while she was on the phone.

'Yes, Sir…I understand.' She said as she held the phone to her ear while her eyes. 'We're simply attempting to verify that something did cross the northern sky…Yes, I know.…I understand, but this is important to our university in regards to astronomical research.'

Cal leaned against the wall of Jess' cubical. Jess shifted positions in her chair in a frustrated fashion.

'We'll take anything, Sir…' She attempted to contain her temper. 'I know…I know, maybe we'll do that. Yeah…thanks.' She dropped the phone on her desk and turned to Cal.

'Do you believe that?' She exclaimed. 'The airport gave me nothing and referred me to the Air Force. That was them…Colonel Wilmont said that there was nothing he could tell us!'

'Well…' Cal replied moving more into Jess' cube. 'He didn't say that they didn't see anything. More than likely, he wouldn't reveal what he may know.'

'Can you believe it?' She replied while shaking her head. 'It's not like we're some guy down on Main Street calling. They know we have the best telescopes and types of radar…and we must have seen something to make such a contact.'

'Hey,' Cal said while opening the large envelope he held. 'Let's take a look at the scope shots.' He handed the envelope to her and leaned in for a closer look.

Jess leafed through the four pictures quickly. "Wow…not much to go on. You can definitely see something, but it's non-distinct and slightly blurry.'

'Basically, just a white spot.' Cal replied studying one of the pictures. 'But…it is there and that proves that we saw something, even as indistinct as it is. There is no way anyone can say that it's a star or comet…its distinct enough to rule that out.'

'Yeah, I guess. It's something…they can't say we didn't see this.' Jess answered.

'Let's take these to Hogan.' Cal replied. 'We have to keep him updated.' They placed the photographs into the envelope and walked down the hallway towards Professor Hogan's office. They passed several photos and paintings of astronomical interest on their walk, but they had a feeling that the pictures they carried possibly meant more to science.

The professor was packing his brief case at the end of the day when Cal and Jess approached his door. He looked up from his task and grinned. 'I bet the two of you have had an interesting afternoon? I see that you have the scope shots too.'

Cal and Jess walked slowly into the room. 'Yes, Professor,' Jess started. 'The pictures prove that there was something in the northern sky that night.'

The professor ran his hand through his hair and sighed. 'Okay...let's have a look.' He gingerly took the envelope from Jess, opened it and leafed through the four 8x10 photographs. 'Well,' He finally uttered. 'It's a light in the sky...four pictures of it. Does it show anything? Not really. Prove anything? No.' He dropped the photos on his desk and looked directly at his two employees.

Cal cleared his throat. 'It proves that something was there...and not moving. It's not a star or a planet.'

Professor Hogan's head shot up. 'Yes, Professor,' Jess jumped in. 'Those shots were taken in a three minute span...and it's in the exact same location...same coordinates throughout.'

The professor ran his hand through his hair again. 'Did the radar system pick up anything?'

'Yes, very faint, but it did.' Cal replied.

'The airport...the Air Force? What did you find out?' He asked.

Jess shook her head. 'The airport didn't want to answer our questions and referred us to the Air Force. Colonel Wilmont of the Air Force had *nothing to tell us*...his words.'

Professor Hogan stood up and walked over towards the white board. He appeared to review his work. 'So, what you have is an interesting sighting...but we have no external confirmation of it. I don't think we have anything to go on.' He turned and faced them. 'I suggest that we just drop it and get back to our normal duties. Besides, it may never appear again.'

Cal and Jess turned and looked at each other. Jess shrugged and rolled her eyes.

'Well, Professor,' Cal said. 'I see your point and we'll put this on the back-burner for now and let you know of any further developments.'

The professor nodded. 'Have a good evening at the scope tonight.'

Shortly thereafter, Jess sat at her station as her shift began. She reviewed notes taken by the previous shift and Cal noticed her somber manner and slowly approached. 'Hey…there is nothing more that we could do with the professor. You know how he gets…we need more proof to have him show some interest.'

She nodded as Cal patted her shoulder. 'Why don't you put some music on…you know how music puts you in a good mood.'

She chuckled. 'Do you really think I need to be cheered up or something?'

'I don't know. You do seem a little introspective.' He replied while gently moving a few items around on her desk. 'When is your CD going to be cut?

'I don't know…it was supposed to be soon, but I haven't heard. I have to have my mom call the agent.'

Cal winced. 'Keep working on the tunes, girl. Practice…a lot of practice… makes perfect…or at least better.' He laughed nervously and moved back towards his desk.

'Huh??' She said as he walked away.

'Hey,' He replied as he turned back towards her. 'Speaking not of rock and roll, but of "rock"…we need to take a look at the moon rock. You know, it did glow while we were viewing the object?'

Jess' head jumped up from her task. 'Oh, man! You're right! I totally forgot about the rock. Let's run it through a scan.'

'Yeah, I agree,' Cal answered. 'I'll have Jergel perform a scan tonight. It'll take a day or so for the scan to complete. I'll brief him about it now.' Jess smiled. 'Yeah, in the meantime, I will take a peek at the northern sky tonight…just in case.'

CHAPTER 6

In 2007, the Arecibo Observatory reported a burst of radio waves from outer space. Since then, the radio waves have been detected at least six additional times.

After an uneventful night, Jess reported for work the following evening with plans to scrutinize the analysis of the moon rock. She was disappointed to find that Jergel had a planned vacation day and wasn't able to fully complete the scan.

Several hours into their shift, as the clock struck one, Cal awoke from a routine induced trance. 'Hey…look at this.' He said as he pointed to his radar screen. 'Something is moving rapidly in the same location as the other night.'

Jess stopped her typing and moved to her screen. 'Yeah! Let's take a look. Moving scope north to northeast!'

'Okay…dome retraction going full visual.' Cal said. 'Synchronizing scope tracing to object coordinates.'

'Looking good…looking good.' Jess replied.

'Talking about me, girl?' Cal answered with a smile.

'You have your days.' She chuckled.

'Maybe I should have shaved today. We're on target…you should have visual.'

'Locking scope on coordinates…got it! Welcome back, baby! It's the same type of object…maybe the same one!'

'Radar still showing confirmation.' Cal uttered. 'I'm recording the radar pattern from origination.' He slowly moved a lever forward. 'Object now at a stand-still. Same coordinates as last time.'

Jess worked feverously at her keyboard. 'I wish the Professor were here. He'd change his mind quickly.'

Cal grunted and shook his head. 'Sorry, Jess, I'm not even sure Professor Hog would believe something he sees with his own eyes.'

'Going for camera scope shots in three!' Jess said as she spun in her chair to another section of her workstation. 'It's a clear night and we should get better resolution.'

'Use maximum zoom, Jess.'

'Going for maximum now…scope shot coming up shortly. Whoaaa!! Max zoom showing colored lights! Red…yellowish white….'

Cal quickly moved to his screen. 'Yes, I'm colorblind and I can see that too. It appears triangular in shape…these pics should be good.'

'Taking them now! One…two…three…it's moving!'

'Yes! Moving west at a rapid speed! Let's adjust the scope.' Cal said excitedly.

'Adjusting!' Jess replied working with passion. 'Moving too fast, though.'

Suddenly, both of their computers issued a loud, audible tone.

'Who is sending us a message at this time?' Jess said.

'Bad timing. No one else is working tonight with Jergel being off. I'll check it.' Cal answered. 'What the hell is this? This is bizarre!'

'What is it?' Jess' head turned quickly towards him.

'It's a message, but I don't know from whom. There's no source.' Cal replied.

'What does it say, Cal?'

'It's binary…it's a string of numbers…01,01,000,01 and it keeps going on in that pattern.'

By the time that they turned their heads towards their screens again, the object was gone.

Shortly after their second encounter with the unidentified object, the two astronomers sat motionless in their chairs.

'Are you okay, Jess?' Cal asked still staring at his screen.

Jess shook her head as though coming out of her own self-induced trance.

'Yeah…I guess, just trying to decipher the binary code.'

Cal grunted. 'Think you can figure out where it's from?'

She sighed. 'Not really…it makes no sense. Not even sure why we picked it up. What about you? Have any thoughts?'

He nodded and grinned. He pointed to the open dome and to the sky. Jess looked up at the gaping hole and into the night sky. 'You mean that you think it came from…the object?'

'Hard to believe, but, yeah, the signal can't be traced to any other source. The object was overhead at the time…seems logical.'

'Logical?' Jess replied as her head swung in his direction. 'That's a U.F.O.!' She ran both hands through her hair. 'Yes, I said it…I said it!'

Cal sat back and looked at her. 'An unidentified flying object, yes…. and….?'

Jess looked him directly into his eyes. She initially flinched and smiled, but regained her seriousness. 'And…you're saying that it sent us a signal? It tried to contact us?'

'You know, you're kind of cute when your hair is disheveled like that?' He chuckled.

She smiled and looked down and simply shook her head.

'Yes, it's possible, Jess. Why not?'

'Okay, but do you know what that means? The magnitude of it all?' Jess said as she combed her hair with her fingers.

'I'm not thinking that big right now,' Cal answered. 'But, until I find a more plausible explanation, that's a good hypothesis.'

Jess dropped her head into her hands. 'Let me call the airport and the Air Force base. Maybe they'll give us some confirmation this time.'

Cal moved towards his computer. 'Good idea. I'm going to contact some other observatories to see if they picked the object.'

CHAPTER 7

The Vatican operates two observatories – one in Vatican City and another in Arizona, USA

On November 11, 2009, the Vatican began consulting experts to study the possibility of extraterrestrial life and its implication on the Catholic Church.

The following evening, Cal and Jess ran into each other in the observatory parking lot as they arrived at the same time. They smiled at each other and slowly exited their respective SUVs.

'You look tired, girl.' Cal said as he flung his bag over his shoulder.

Jess nodded. 'Yeah…couldn't sleep.'

'I woke up a few times myself, but I did get a few good hours in.' Cal replied.

Jess sipped her coffee. 'I think that it was partly due to not receiving any replies from the airport or Air Force last night. It's frustrating…and I'm worried that they think that we're a little off of our rockers.'

'Can't say that it doesn't concern me a little too.' He answered. 'Maybe we'll find out that they replied today. It was the middle of the night when you contacted them.'

'We'll see…' She said as they entered the lobby. They were soon greeted by Bob Breyer, one of the day light shift astronomers.

'Hey, Jergel has been waiting to see you all day. He keeps rambling on and on about that moon rock.' Breyer said.

'Really?' Jess replied. 'We'll put our gear in our cubes and head to the lab.'

'If you have time, Bob, why don't you meet us there?' Cal said. 'I'm sure that you'll find it interesting.'

'Never thought you'd ask.' He smiled. 'I'll stop in.'

Cal and Jess walked quickly towards their cubicles. Cal looked around them as he walked. 'Jergel must have found something really interesting. He's not really excitable…a little weird, but not excitable'

Jess agreed. 'Not sure how much more excitement I can take.'

'Then I'll be sure to keep my distance from you. You know my magnetism.' He chuckled.

'You do that.' She laughed as they walked into the research lab and met Jergel at his desk.

'Dudes…I'm glad you're here.' The young researcher, sporting a brown-spiked hair style, replied. 'That rock of yours…don't know what to make of it. Follow me to the table and I'll show you.'

Cal and Jess gave each other a questioning glance and immediately followed. 'How many energy drinks have you had today, Jergs?' Cal asked with a smirk. 'You're not just seeing things again…are you?' He winked at Jess, just as Bob Breyer entered the lab.

'Dudes…I'm telling you, I'm lost here.' Jergel replied without breaking his stride. He stopped at the table and began to put on a pair of surgical-type gloves. He placed the rock under bright, LED lighting and focused a camera right at the rock's center. The three astronomers gathered around the table.

'Check out the magnified screen.' Jergel said. 'First, look at the rock's surface…the texture. Now, here is another moon rock on the second screen. Check out the differences.'

'They are not even close.' Breyer said while intensely scanning each screen.

'No, they're not.' Jergel answered.

'Do you have some pics of other types of moon rocks?' Jess asked. 'There are several types.'

Jergel worked his keyboard. 'Yeah, that was the closest match, but here are all of the known types and the same magnification of each. Dudes… not one is similar. There are no matches.'

Cal rubbed his chin. 'Hmm…any theory, Jergs?'

He sighed heavily and shook his head. 'If this is a moon rock, it's really rare.'

'It looks to be that way,' Cal answered while still reviewing the screens. 'But, the *Apollo* missions generally took the rocks from the same locations. How one could be so different is intriguing.'

'Did you run a particle or geological analysis?' Jess asked.

'Yeah, here...take a look.' He handed her a sheet of paper from within a folder. 'The analysis showed that it has very few common properties with other moon rocks.'

'You're kidding?' Breyer blurted.

'No, dudes...this rock must be from the dark side of the moon or something.'

After several additional minutes of discussion, Cal and Jess took their leave to begin their shift.

'What's up with that rock?' Jess asked as they walked towards the scope room. 'Things are starting to freak me out.'

'It's definitely odd...I'll give you that, Jess, but I'll have Jergel run a few more analytics on it before I go to the Professor with this information.'

Jess mockingly laughed. 'Jergel may actually already have. He has a tough time keeping secrets. Hey, I didn't want to mention it to him, but we never brought up the fact that we saw the rock glow.'

'I know,' Cal replied. 'I figured we would see if he came up with something on his own about that. Once he was baffled, I didn't want to throw another curve at him right then. I'll bring it up to him soon.'

Cal and Jess went through their night-shift routine, which included logging in to various computer systems. Jess immediately checked her messages for the day.

'Do you believe it? The airport claims it has 'No confirmation of any odd sightings' and the Air Force base is simply not responding to my inquiry!'

Cal sat down at his workstation. 'Honestly, doesn't surprise me. Let me check the observatory sites to see if there is any chatter today.'

'Yeah...any news is better than none.' Jess sighed.

'Hmmm. Nothing much on here...hard to believe. Just your normal stuff. Hold on! Here's something from...of all places...Arecibo!!'

'Arecibo!!' Jess jumped from her seat and moved towards Cal's station.

'Yes, it appears that they have confirmed the possibility of a faint signal from an unknown source. Let me see when and where. Hey, same time... same location as when we viewed the object.'

'The signal, Cal! We received the digital signal!'

'Wow! Yes, we did, girlfriend.' His eyes lit up and they casually embraced. Cal quickly withdrew back to his seat, not noticing Jess' wide smile.

'This is awesome, though.' He said as he scrolled through his screen. 'I see no other confirmations of the signal from anyone else. There are quite a few comments and follow-ups from the Arecibo post, but no one else is giving an original report.'

'That report, in itself, will make news.' Jess said as she returned to her seat. 'Arecibo is searching for signals from outer space as a radio telescope, which they apparently received. That may explain why they were the only other recipients.'

'But, we are the only ones that appear to have a visual of the object.' Cal replied while still scanning his screens.

'Speaking of the visual,' Jess replied as she adjusted several dials. "I'm going to pick up the new scope shots when I come in tomorrow.'

'Yeah, those should be more definitive this time.' Cal said.

Jess turned to face him. 'Well, what if they are? What do we do then?'

Cal shrugged. 'We have to go through the chain of command...Hogan... the University President...then receive clearance to go beyond that point.'

The next evening, the two astronomers arrive for their shift and were summoned into Professor Hogan's office. Upon their arrival, they found Hogan sitting at his desk and he appeared to be dismayed and disheveled. He wasted little time in informing them that their scope shots had been confiscated. Supposedly, the Air Force arrived in the morning and requested the pictures directly through the University President. He complied without hesitation.

'I never saw the photos, but I did protest that action…in the name of science…for astronomy.' Hogan stated as he hit his fist on the desk. 'But, the University's hands were tied…many federally funded projects were at stake, as you know.'

'This is outrageous!' Jess exclaimed almost slamming her hand on the desk also. 'That was University property and possibly of great scientific and historical value!'

'The latter reason is why they took them, Jess.' Cal replied surprisingly calmly. 'When history isn't recorded…is it truly history?'

'Dam it!!' Jess blurted without remorse. 'I'm calling Colonel Wilmont myself and giving him a large piece of my mind! How dare they interfere in our operations…it sickens me!'

Professor Hogan sighed. 'I understand your frustration, Jess…I really do. Though, I have to point out that it wasn't military personnel from the base that came here. Actually, I'm not even certain they were military at all.'

'What do you mean, Professor?' Cal asked.

'They were not in military uniforms, but stated that they were from some investigative unit of the Air Force. They showed the proper credentials and all…they were definitely Federal.'

'Were the credentials checked?' Cal replied.

'The President had his staff contact the base to verify that they were supposed to be here…before releasing the photos.' Hogan answered.

Cal sat down in one of the chairs in front of the Professor's desk. 'We're definitely onto something here. Professor, did they happen to be wearing black suits…by any chance?'

The Professor sat up straight with interest. 'Yes, in fact, they did.'

Cal shook his head. 'The notorious "Men in Black." Yeah, if this incident has them involved they'll try to keep everything under the radar as much as possible. We'll never see those scope shots again.'

They reluctantly returned to their cubes and Jess flung herself into her desk chair. 'Do you believe it? They just walk in here and basically rob us! This is really getting out of control...it really is.'

Cal walked into her personal space and leaned against her desk. 'Hey, we are onto something here or else they wouldn't have taken the scope shots. We, as scientists, have come across a possible significant breakthrough and we should, at least, take some solace in that.'

Jess nodded slightly. 'Maybe...not sure we'll ever find out, though. Let alone be credited for it.'

'True.' He replied. 'But, we are only doing our job and we'll continue to do so. 'Here,' Cal said as he pushed the "on" button on her CD player. 'Relax and listen to some of your favorite Tony Bennett songs...you know, before we go to work again.'

Jess' eyes closed as the music came on. She leaned her head against the back of her chair. 'His voice is so soothing.'

'Yeah,' Cal quickly replied. 'He's in his 80's and his voice is better than many younger female singers.'

Jess' eyes popped open. Huh? Did you say something about *younger female* singers?'

Cal calmly faked a yawn and rubbed his eyes. 'Whaaa? No...no...I said male *and* female...I mean...he's just good...regardless of age...yeah.' Jess stoically watched him casually stroll back to his cube.

That same evening, the two astronomers find themselves in their workstations preparing for yet another shift of measuring the distances between stars. Their work had also played a major role in discovering another earth-like planet and they were dedicated to their task. While deep into their work, Jergel, who happened to be working late, approached them.

'Hey, dudes, I know that you've seen some bizarre objects recently, but look at this on the local news site.' He said as he approached carrying a tablet computer. 'The Air Force is saying that they have been testing new aircraft in the area. They said that this should explain any odd sightings.'

'What!?' Jess sneered as she turned towards him. 'Is that what they're putting out there?'

'Looks like it, Jess. Basically front page news.' He replied.

'That's bull-shit!' Cal murmured. 'It looks like they are trying to create a cover story. The odd part about this whole thing is that *we* are the only ones who have seen it. There are no other reports of the sighting... anywhere.'

'I guess they're doing this in case someone else did.' Jess said.

'This further proves the validity of the sighting.' Cal answered. 'Jergs... do us a favor and place that moon rock in a small, glass display case and put it on that table in the corner.'

'Sure...sure. I'm not totally done with my analysis, but I want that out of my lab anyway. I'm not sure even what it is...freaks me out, you know? I'll bring it up on my way out...have to find an empty case first.'

CHAPTER 8

In May 2016, NASA's Kepler Space Telescope confirmed 1,284 newly discovered planets. Thousands of additional planets are expected to be discovered in the near future.

The next day, Cal and Jess receive a message to report to Professor Hogan's office upon arriving for work. Not knowing what to expect, they arrive early and meet outside the Professor's office.

'Kind of tired of reporting to "Hog-land"…aren't you?' Cal asked as they walked in the door.

Professor Hogan briefly greeted them and directed them to a side table that held his large screen computer. 'First, take a look at today's paper.' He said as he unfolded it on the table and pointed to the headline. The headline read: *No Unidentified Objects in Local Skies*

He then pointed to the sub-headings of the article: *Air Force testing aircraft, contrary to university claims*

'What is this?' Jess exclaimed picking up the paper. 'We saw something online last night and I checked for updates today, but who spoke to the media?'

'We've been avoiding them all day, Jess.' Professor Hogan replied with arms out-stretched. 'Since, we didn't give them an interview they went to the Air Force and even the Airport Authority for details. Hell, even the FAA chimed in. Here…look at the local news website.' He touched his computer keyboard and the large screen lit and displayed a similar headline.

'We never went to the media, Professor.' Cal said. 'If we didn't, who did?'

The Professor strolled around the room shaking his head. 'They did…the Air Force did…or those Men in Black. They are trying to end speculation here and now.'

Cal ran his hand through his hair and also began to stroll. 'At the same time, they are discrediting us.'

'Hmmph!!' Professor Hogan blurted. 'The university President is not happy to say the least. He called me into his office earlier today to directly inform me of that.'

Jess leaned against a wall. 'What are we supposed to do at this point? Just pretend it didn't happen?'

The Professor turned to her with hands on hips. 'Jess, you see that they want to discredit the university, which could be disastrous with all of our federally funded research...and projects. I know that you don't want to hear this...but the President wants this subject to go away.'

Cal moaned softly. 'Okay...Okay...we can do that. From now on this is a covert operation, Professor. No more contacts outside of the observatory...everyone fine with that?'

The Professor looked him directly in the eye and nodded. 'It better be *very* covert...understand? They'll discredit you personally next. Cal, you've always dreamed of a Nobel Prize...or having a celestial object named after you.' He shook his head. 'You have talent, but it will never happen if this continues...you know that. Heck, you may even lose your chance to work for NASA again.'

Cal hung his head and nodded softly. Without further discussion, he and Jess left the office.

That same night, while comfortably seated at her workstation, Jess' head rises slowly to an audible signal emanating from an overhead monitor. 'Whooaa....wow!! Slow down, baby!' She exclaimed and immediately jumped to the scope controls. 'Cal!! Heads-up!!'

Cal dropped his *Astronomy* magazine on his desk and begins to scan his monitors. 'Watcha got?'

'Covert operation in effect my man.' She replied not looking at him. 'We have company...again.'

'No choice but to deal with it.' He said with a slight smile. 'Scope tracking is on.'

'Heading to the same location...and a dead stop!' She answers in amazement. 'It's like it has its own parking spot in the sky.'

'Zoom, girlfriend, zoom!!' Cal barks.

'Zooming…maximum zoom in ten seconds. FYI, I'm not your girlfriend.' She cracks a quick smile in his direction.

He returns the smile before returning to the monitors. 'It's definitely a ship. It's very clear and the best view that we've had. Not one of ours either, regardless of what they say. We don't have aircraft that that can fly that fast and can stop on the dime…new technology or otherwise.'

Jess sighs loudly. 'I could just cry.'

'Hold it together there.' He replies quickly. 'Let's get the job done. You know, we're the few, the proud…the Space Cadets, etc.'

She chuckles. 'It's a clear night and that's helping with the view. Look! There are the colors again around the base. I'm initiating scope shots.'

'Yes, fire away. We'll develop them in the university lab…I know a guy that will help.'

'Scope shots in fifteen seconds…on auto.' She says while pressing a large, red button on her control panel.

Suddenly, another audible tone echoes through the cavernous room. Digits begin to appear on their computer screens.

'Cal! The numerical code again!'

'I see it…and copying it down!'

'What do you think it is?' She replies doing the same.

'Not sure, but I'm running a high intensity security and virus scan on the systems starting now.' He leans over and types on his keyboard. 'It's possible that they are downloading our databases.'

Jess nodded. 'Good thinking, but I can't imagine what they would want from us or could be searching for. Let me know if you need a system shut down. FYI – I have three incredible scope shots in the books.'

'Bravo!' Cal said without stopping his work. 'It's possible that 'they' are here for a reason and not just lost. They could be gathering information or much, much more. Please place the scope on high speed auto tracking and check the feeds to see if anyone has a visual.'

'Will do.' Jess answered. 'Though, I've had my screen on the feeds all night and there have not been any updates....no chatter.'

Cal smacked his hand on the desk. 'Do you know what that means? They are basically trying to communicate with us...and *only* us! We really have to decipher that code, but I hope that they know that humans don't normally communicate in numbers. Look, Jess!' He says suddenly. 'Something else is appearing on screen...very faintly!'

Jess moved closer to her screen. 'It's some kind of picture or graphic. Hey, I've seen this before.'

Cal stood up to get a closer view of the screen. 'Do you know what this is? These are the graphics from the plates that appeared on the Pioneer missions in the early 70's!'

'Do you mean the ones that were to explain earth and humankind to extraterrestrial life forms?' Jess asked.

'Exactly! It looks like they are projecting the plates on our screens... incredible. The Pioneer spacecrafts, both *Pioneer 10* and *Pioneer 11*, contained a pictorial message in case they were intercepted by extraterrestrial life.' Cal replied as he stared in astonishment at his screen. 'Maybe...they finally have.'

'Oh, wow! What are you saying?' Jess answered as she swung towards him in her chair. 'This is just hitting me over the head now...I mean... wow!'

'Great scientific response, my girl.' Cal said with a smirk. 'I know...it's astonishing to comprehend now, but I don't have a different hypothesis at the current time.'

Jess seemed a little annoyed, but returned the smirk. 'Sorry, I can't contain my excitement or emotions at times...even in times like these.'

'Not to worry, Jess...we're not robots, but let's stay focused, because this could be big.' Cal began to work his keyboard. 'Hey, the graphic is beginning to fade from the screen...check the scope please.'

'Scope shows that they are moving...northwest at a high rate of speed!' Jess replied. 'They'll be out of range in five seconds.'

'Let'em go.' Cal said still working the keyboard. 'I have a strong feeling we haven't seen the last of them. Let's have Olivia run an algorithm scan of this code.' Cal said as he prepared an email with the code attached. 'We might be able to decipher it.'

'It's communicative...that's how I see it.' Jess answered.

'Yes, but when Arecibo first came online in 1974 it sent out a similar coded message into space...digital...in hopes of getting a response. I need to know if it's the same message or different. We'll check to see if they picked up a message again too.'

Jess nodded. 'Either way, I still can't figure out how it appeared on our screens.'

Suddenly, the door to the control room burst open and Jergel hesitantly came in. He held a small glass case in his hands.

'Jergs...we're in the middle of another "event" if you can believe it.' Cal said as he peaked over his shoulder.

'You want an event?' He answered. 'Dude, look at this!'

Cal and Jess turned in their chairs almost simultaneously. They saw Jergel holding the glass case out in front of him, which contained the glowing moon rock. 'What the hell is this, Dude? It's a freakin glowing rock!' Jergel said as he was clearly uncomfortable holding the object.

'Okay, Jergs...stay calm. Just put it down on the desk right there.' Cal replied slowly walking towards him. Jergel immediately moved towards the desk and was happy to deposit the case in the specified location. He slowly backed away from the object.

'Dude, what is that?' He said as he turned to Cal.

'Well, we're not certain. It appears to glow like that when we have an incident. I was going to mention it to you, Jergs…it skipped my mind. Sorry.'

'I had that in my lab for a week…I might be radioactive or something now, Dude.' He wiped his mouth with his hand and stared at the object in disdain.

'No worries…we checked that…as you did, if you recall.' Cal said as he walked over to the case.

'Oh, yeah…still freaks me out, though. You owe me a drink for that… no, six freakin drinks, Dude.'

'You got it, Jergs.' Cal replied with a smirk. 'Hey, why don't you help us look at a code? See if you can figure it out.'

'Yeah, yeah…sure. I'm going back down to my lab. Send it to me.' He replied as he quickly left the room.

Jess and Cal stood over the glowing rock. 'Check it out!' Jess said in amazement. 'This is truly incredible.'

'We need to talk to Mr. Painter. Something tells me there is more to the story about this rock than we know.' Cal said as he checked the rock with a large magnifying glass.

Jess agreed. 'Let's visit him tomorrow then.'

CHAPTER 9

July 2014 - NASA states that as many as 100 million worlds exist in the Milky Way Galaxy (alone) and may be home to alien life.

The following day was the autumn day of all autumn days. Bright, crisp, clear to the point where a hint of apple cider was in the air. Cal and Jess had arranged a meeting with Mr. Painter to discuss the moon rock beyond what was relayed to them when they obtained it. They met him at his shop and he offered them a seat at an antique table near the window. 'Thanks for meeting us again, Mr. Painter.' Cal said as he opened a notepad. 'We would like to ask a few questions about the moon rock, such as where you obtained it?'

'I told you where I obtained it. I'm not in any kind of trouble…am I?' He replied leaning forward in his seat.

'No, not that we're aware of and we are not here for that reason. Please, be frank with us and tell us everything that you know, including the exact location of where you found it.'

Mr. Painter nodded. 'Well, you see, I did find the rock…but, it wasn't in the Rocky Mountains as I had originally stated. I found it overseas.'

'Overseas?' Jess asked. 'Where exactly?'

'Well, earlier this year the wife wanted to take a trip across the pond to Ireland.' He rubbed his chin. 'She's into St. Patrick's Day and Irish lore…you know. She's Irish…I appeased her and went. I figured that I might be able to pick up a few unique items for the store as well. One day, towards the end of the trip, we were actually at an antique store on the western coastline of Ireland. As we were leaving, we noticed that there was a hiking trail right near the shop that took you along the coastline. We headed for the trail and about fifteen minutes later we were right there…on the coast. Beautiful…it was a very rocky area…water was a little rough, etc. We decided to walk another five minutes and then turn around and go back. As we did, I noticed…"the moon rock"…up ahead about ten yards off the path. It stood out…it was very, very different than all of the other rocks. I left the path to take a closer look and I could tell that it was unique. I'm into unique, so I picked it up and placed it into my satchel that I happen to carry on trips. My wife protested…but, that'll get her nowhere.' He laughed. 'Hey, after all, I went on this trip for her and she has to let me get something out of it too…you know what I mean?' He chuckled again. 'There you have it - that's how the rock came into the store.'

Cal cleared his throat. 'I see…so, the rock is from Ireland. Is that why you didn't state that earlier?'

Mr. Painter Grunted. 'Yes, you can see why I wouldn't. I was terrified of getting it through customs.'

'I can see that.' Cal said. 'What did you think the rock was when you picked it up? What made it unique?'

'It was odd in color, texture and even a little in shape. Just didn't seem to be normal rock. I had seen pictures of moon rocks and had a slight inclination that it could be one…or more so a meteorite or something. More so, as I mentioned, I do have a large rock and mineral collection and this was certainly nothing that I had encountered previously.'

'As long as you owned the rock, did you notice anything odd about it… in anyway?' Jess replied.

'No, not at all. It was kept in box in the backroom up until I took it out for display the week that you happened to walk in.' He looked towards Cal. 'I was pretty sure, after researching it more, that it was not of this earth, but was never sure until the geologist looked at it the last time you were here.'

CHAPTER 10

Per astronomers on the PBS series *NOVA*, there are more stars in the universe than there are grains of sand on every beach on Earth… combined. Approximately 70 percent of the stars have orbiting planets.

'Hey, Jess,' Cal said while reading a text message. 'Olivia has run some code breaking programs against the digital code. She said that she'll be here in the library in a minute.'

Jess peaked up from behind her laptop screen and glasses with the revelation of the news. 'Sounds good.' She answered returning to her work. 'Glad we came in early this afternoon to do our "Off-The-Record" research. I'm really getting some things done…surprisingly. If Olivia is coming in…that will be good news too.'

A soft knock soon was heard at the door and a young brunette entered the brightly lit observatory library without waiting for a reply.

'Hey, girl,' Jess said, again peeking out from behind her screen. 'What'cha got good?'

The well-dressed Olivia returned the greeting, sat across from them and opened her tablet computer. 'Well, I ran algorithms and various code-breaking programs against the…very bizarre, digital code. In digital code…the only word that can be derived from it…in a basic format…is "no." I've ordered a more extensive algorithm program from the university's Computer Science Department and it should be here tomorrow. I'm hoping that will reveal other verbiage.'

Cal sat up straight. 'Hmm. Odd that such a long code results in only a two-letter word.'

Olivia cleared her throat. 'I agree and that's why I've ordered the other program. It's also possible that the code does not contain a verbiage-type message.'

'If it's not wording, what else could it be?' Jess replied. 'We could be at a dead-end.'

Cal stood and paced slowly behind his chair. 'Let's face it…the source of this code, in my opinion, comes from a life form…forms… much more advanced than ours. It has to be more advanced or else it couldn't possibly have traveled this far. They have scientific knowledge that we can only dream of.'

Jess and Olivia exchanged glances.

'Considering that, "they" know what we can and cannot decipher...it can be assumed. I'm certain of that.'

'So, you're saying that we keep trying to break the code?' Jess answered quizzically. 'I doubt that we would have given up anyway.'

'We wouldn't have, Jess.' He replied. 'But, we should think outside of the box...so, to speak.'

'Where should we start then?' Olivia asked. 'I'll start with the new program when I receive it, but do you have another theory?'

Cal stopped his pacing and leaned on the back of his chair. 'If it's not a verbiage code...it may be a numerical code.'

'A numerical code?' Jess said while removing her glasses. 'The numbers actually may translate to... numbers?'

'Not necessarily a pure numerical code...it still has to be translated.' Cal replied looking her directly in the eye. 'My theory is that they could be coordinates.'

'Coordinates?' Jess replied. 'To what?'

Cal began to pace again. 'To some "place" here on the planet. Possibly, they are looking for a specific location.'

Jess chuckled. 'You said that they were advanced! Hell, with my GPS and Google I can find anyplace on Earth! What's their issue?'

Cal nodded and laughed. 'That's something for us to find out and we'll go from there. Olivia, when you get the new program, include a coordinate search.'

Olivia nodded and jotted it down. 'Can't wait to give it a whirl.' She replied smiling.

Near his nightly workstation, Cal stood over the glass-encased "moon" rock, peering at it as though a clue that a microscopic analysis may have missed and could now be discerned with the naked eye. His eyes covered the entire width and length, but his only reaction was to shake his head.

'Notice something?' Jess asked as she entered the room for her shift.

'Unfortunately…not.' He replied. 'There has to be a clue here. I mean, it does glow when the object appears.'

'I think that we know there is some correlation, don't we? We also know that Jergel is too freaked out to analyze it any further.' She said as she took her seat.

'Yeah, he's a weasel.' Cal replied. 'I may have to drive this over to the university labs for more information.'

'Wouldn't they love that?' Jess said.

'You need to love something…and that would be it for them…a conundrum just like this. They would buy me beers for a year.' He smiled.

'We all need to love something.' She also smiled sheepishly and looked briefly in his direction. 'Don't you think?'

'Yeah…sure.' He nodded.

The door to the room opened and Professor Hogan's voice was soon heard.

'Cal…Jess? Have a minute?'

'Bad timing, Professor.' Jess mumbled.

'What was that? He replied. 'Am I interrupting something?'

'No…No…come in, Professor.' Cal answered as he turned from the rock and began to walk towards the door. 'What can we do for you?'

The Professor stopped at Cal's station and paused. 'Just checking on your "informal" research project. I've been reading your email reports, but the President wants an update.'

Cal nodded. 'Glad to see that there is some interest. Well, it's moving along, so to speak. We've done some code analysis and we're following up on that right now with Olivia. We've interviewed the dealer who sold the rock to the university.' He said as he pointed in the rock's direction. 'Seems as though it's from good old Ireland.'

'Ireland?' The Professor replied as he slowly sauntered in the rock's direction. 'That's interesting. Is this…thing…still glowing?'

Jess cleared her throat. 'Oh, yeah, Professor, every time we see something move in the heavens. It has a *lovely* glow, actually.' She smiled at Cal. 'It really gives the room ambiance. If I could manufacture them we'd make a fortune on QVC.'

Cal shot her a look and then smiled.

The Professor stood peering into the glass case. 'This thing freaks me out.'

'You aren't the only one around here that feels that way.' Cal replied as he walked up beside him. 'No worries…it doesn't move.'

'I know…I know.' Professor Hogan answered. 'You know, the military is calling here everyday…asking questions…wanting our nightly reports.'

Cal looked back at Jess. 'Don't worry, we've held off on providing more information. The President doesn't like that they are trying to intimidate us, especially since this observatory is in the business of discovering celestial objects. He made some calls to the Governor's office, as well as the Senator's office and Federal Representatives. They, in turn, have made some inquiries…contacted the Pentagon…and things are a little quieter right now.'

Cal began to pace. 'Professor, what do you think that they know about these sightings? Do you believe that they know more than we do and are just trying to bury the whole thing?'

The Professor crossed his arms. 'I don't think that they know anything. That's why they keep coming here for information. Don't get me wrong… they are aware that something is appearing. They don't know what it is and they don't like the fact that you've noticed it also…and may know more about it than they do.'

Cal stopped in his tracks. 'So, you believe that we are the leading authority in regards to this issue?'

The Professor nodded. 'I'd say so. They're trying to create a cover story with smoke and mirrors.'

'I guess if they wanted to they could shut us down.' Jess interjected.

'Exactly.' The Professor answered. 'But they haven't. They haven't because we have more information than they do.'

Cal nodded. 'From what we've seen from reading the observatory feeds, we may be the only ones with real information. We'll keep at it then… we'll keep looking to the stars, Professor.'

CHAPTER 11

Bolstered by recent discoveries, on April 8, 2015, NASA scientists stated that they believe they could find evidence of alien life (conservatively) by 2025.

'Are you kidding me, Olivia?' Cal stated as he stared at an information filled report. 'You are kidding me?'

Olivia bowed her head for a second and then looked him directly in the eye. 'I wish that I was, but…no.'

'Really?' Was his only reply.

'Look, Cal, the code translation program came back with that…those statements. Are they 50, 75, 100 percent accurate…who knows?'

Their colleague, Bob Breyer, who was also in the library, grunted in agreement. 'My guess, at best, is that it is ballpark jargon.'

Cal shook his head. 'This is unbelievable.' He couldn't take his eyes from the report.

'Are you going to let me read it?' Jess exclaimed. 'Don't keep all of the excitement to yourself.'

Cal popped out of his self-induced trance, shook his head and handed her the report. 'Girl, you need to read this. It appears that they even refer to themselves as…*One*.'

Jess took the report and read the code translation aloud.

One is in search of probe.

Location is non-compatible to One's needs.

She put the report down with an astonished look. 'Wow! I mean… Whoaaa! Absolutely incredible!'

Olivia spoke up. 'Again, we are not certain of its accuracy. These code translation programs were never intended to decipher an…alien…code. Can I say that?'

Cal sat down. 'Yes, the programs were never intended for the purpose, but, the most common "universal" language…if one would exist on a true universal scale, would be binary. I actually did research on that subject at NASA.'

Jess nodded. 'Can't argue with that.'

'I would agree too. It's a given that numerical writing would be the most common used in any aspect of civilization.' Breyer replied.

'So, we can agree that there could be some credence to the translation then?' Olivia asked.

'In theory, yes.' Cal answered. 'Hey, not to take the subject in a new direction, but we were also interested in the code being a possible coordinate to a location. Did anything come up?'

Olivia opened the folder in front of her and extracted another document. 'As a matter of fact…yes. The programs that we ran it through came back with a specific location, based on longitude and latitude points.' She brushed her hair behind her ears. 'It's an odd location, though, in a body of water…not far from the British Isles.'

Cal sat up in his chair. 'The British Isles? Did I hear you correctly?'

'Yes, actually, more off the coast of Ireland…I should say. The southwest coast to be exact.' She pulled a map out of her folder and spread it across the large, oak table. 'Here, I charted it the location on this map.'

The group gathered around as she pointed to the location that she determined.

Cal pointed his pen from the specified location to the Irish mainland. 'What some of you may not know is that the antiquities dealer who sold the rock to the university, said that he found it approximately…right here.' He pointed to the furthest southwest corner of Ireland.

'Seriously?' Breyer said as he moved closer to the map.

'Yes, that's what he told us and we have no reason to question that.' Cal answered without removing his gaze from the location.

'Well, the coordinates are in the Atlantic Ocean.' Olivia said. 'Again, if they are accurate.'

'If they are a little off they could be at the southwestern point of Ireland.' Breyer answered.

'That would be a perfect fit, wouldn't it be?' Cal said.

'This is amazing.' Jess replied while moving her finger back and forth between the two locations on the map.

'I'm interested,' Cal said. 'If there is anything specific about these locations...the location in the Atlantic and even where the rock was found. We can perform some internet searches.'

'Why don't we contact the geography department...maybe even the history department?' Breyer said. 'They may some information.'

'Yeah, maybe Professor Walker will give us a lead. I'm on it.' Jess replied as she headed to her computer.

CHAPTER 12

Since 1959, a non-profit research organization called the Search for Extraterrestrial Intelligence (SETI) has scanned the skies and listened for radio waves in search for other civilizations. NASA has funded SETI projects in the 1960's, 1970's and 1990's. Since its inception, SETI has recorded 400 radio signals, including one in 1977 that lasted 72 seconds, which was determined to fit the profile of a message from another world.

The cool night air crept through as Cal opened the dome. Night fell earlier at this time of year, which made for a few extra hours of freelance sky viewing. Jess ran several system checks, while casually watching Cal move through his routine.

'Hey, Cal…' She suddenly said urgently. 'Man…it looks like it's going to be one of those nights!'

'What's up?' He replied taking a quick glance in her direction.

'Radar shows an anomaly…*again*.' She answered.

'Visitors?' He said stopping his work and moving to his screen.

'Do they actually know when we start our shift or something?' She replied shaking her head.

Cal Laughed. 'I'm sure. "They" have come from light years away…I think clock time is not too hard for them to decipher.'

Jess uttered a nervous laugh. 'I'm convinced we are the only ones they are communicating with.'

Cal looked over at her. 'I agree. I also am inclined to say that we are the only ones that can see them.'

Jess returned his glance. 'Yeah…I keep scanning the feeds and nothing. No chatter…no sightings…just nothing. How is it possible that we can only see them?'

'Haven't you watched *Star Trek*? It's called "cloaking." Basically, they can expose themselves to only those they want to be seen by. Let's get the scope on tracking mode.' Cal said. 'They're close…the rock is starting to glow.'

Jess stood for a better look at the rock in the far corner or the large room. She sighed and scratched her head. 'Okay, scope tracking is on. I'll take more scope shots too. Cloaking, huh?'

'Everything you need to know you can learn from *Star Trek*. There they are.' Cal said. 'Same location…they've stopped.'

'Got it.' Jess replied. 'Where is that location exactly anyway? Can we determine that?'

'You know, we've never looked at that aspect.' Cal replied while moving several levers simultaneously. 'But, that's one of our expertise's here, determining the distances between celestial objects, so maybe we can figure that out. I'm locking onto the location for the purpose.'

'It will be interesting. Once you get a good lock just let me know. I'll run it through the computer and we'll get a coordinate. It may take as long as the planetary measurements, which are several hours to a day, but let's do it.'

'Magnification of the scope is on...nice...nice.' Cal exclaimed. 'It's a great view of the object...the ship...okay, I said it.'

The triangular object appeared in high-definition on their large screen. It emitted several glowing lights on its underside.

'Crazy.' Jess mumbled 'Just crazy. Too bad we can't have people on the other scopes too.'

A tone soon came from the computer system. 'Hey...Hey...may be another message. Same tone as last time.' Cal said excitedly. 'We need to get a screen shot of it if it comes across.'

'Yeah...Yeah, sure.' Jess answered while working her keyboard.

The screens went blank and were soon filled by a stream of digits that engulfed the monitors.

'There! There!' Cal said. 'All ones and zeros again. Binary code.'

'Screen shot being taken...we're good, Cal.'

'Great, I didn't feel like trying to write them all down again like last time. One digit off and it could be interpreted completely differently. Especially in the short time that they seem to appear on screen.'

A few minutes later, the screens went completely blank and returned to their normal functions.

'They're moving. High rate of speed…wow! Already out of radar range…' Cal uttered.

Jess simply sank her head into her hands.

'Let's keep it together, Jess.' Cal said noticing her reaction. 'You did a great job and, if it helps any, as I mentioned before, you look cute with your hair disheveled like that.'

She peaked up from between her hands already sporting a smile.

'You do.' He said smiling. 'I'm emailing this screen shot to Olivia to run through the code breaking program.'

The next afternoon, Cal arranged for a meeting in the observatory's conference room. He invited Jergel to report on the Geology Department's analysis of the rock, Olivia to report on the results of the code breaking program's review of the latest binary code and Jess to report on Professor Walker's geography report on the coordinates from the first message. Bob Breyer was also invited, as was Professor Hogan, who was on his way.

Cal stood and addressed the group. 'Let's start with our glowing rock. Jergs, what do you have for us?'

The disheveled lab director opened his laptop and attached it to a projector. He projected the known moon rock samples on the screen.

'Dude, these are all of the different types of moon rocks that we know of. You've seen this before. These next slides are known pieces of meteorites, etc. The next slides are rocks as they appear on Mars. Now, a team of people in the Geology Department reviewed the rock and compared it to all known celestial rocks of any kind…known to man. Dudes…and Dudettes…that rock doesn't match anyone of them. I mean, not even close…short and simple.'

Cal raised his eyebrows and cleared his throat. 'So, where do they believe it's from?'

Jergel threw up his hands. 'No idea, Dude…from somewhere we've never been before…ask George Jetson…I don't know.'

'Good info actually, Jergs…er…Dude. Thanks.' Cal said. He then turned to Olivia. 'This, I can't wait to hear. What has the program to say about our code from last night?'

The well-dressed programmer put on her glasses and attached her laptop to the projector.

'Well, my friends, this is the same type of binary code as previously received. It's getting interesting. Same program deciphered it and…take a look.' She projected several lines on the screen and then read them aloud.

One is following your probe and ours

One has visited the third planet in the past

Returning for need

Cal sighed loudly and everyone sat up in their chairs.

'Liv, if that's a good translation the program works. That actually makes some sense.' Cal said.

'Yes,' Breyer replied pointing towards the screen. 'They say "Following your probe." That has to be Pioneer crafts that they projected on your screens that one night.'

Cal nodded heavily. 'Yes, that's what crossed my mind too.'

'Now, "their probe"…who knows what is meant by that? Otherwise, it makes sense. They refer to the third planet, which would be Earth…the third planet from the sun.' Breyer said.

'Hey, guys, maybe I have something that could help with that.' Jess said.

Everyone swung their chairs in her direction as she hooked up her laptop to the projector.

'Here are the coordinates from the first message on the screen, but, before we go into detail, check out this article from 1980. It is the Rendlesham Forest incident, which occurred near a U.S. Air Force base in Suffolk, England. She then projected a news report on the screen. 'This is one of the most documented and witnessed UFO sightings in history. What makes it so credible is that it happened on or near an Air Force base and was witnessed by several military personnel. Though they never spoke of the incident during their careers, they have come forward recently. Take a few minutes to read this.'

The group did so and several astonished looks were exchanged. The article stated that military personnel actually touched a small flying object that had landed near the base.

The group was silent as it read the news reports of the incident.

'Well,' Jess finally said. 'As you read, witnesses claimed to have received a telepathic binary code when they touched the object. The code was engrained in their mind…or mind's eye…and they eventually wrote the code down. It almost appears as though the object was attempting to communicate with them. The code that they received was identical… absolutely identical…to one that we received in the first message.'

'So, what are we saying here, Jess?' Breyer asked. 'That the code is from the same source?'

Cal held up his hand. 'Yes, in my opinion, it is. My theory is that it is the same source because not only is it the same message…which would include coordinates…those coordinates match Olivia's analysis placing the location near Ireland…not far from England. It can be assumed that the craft that landed in the Rendlessham Forest is the one that deposited the beacon…the rock.'

'And your glowing rock is from that area, Dude.' Jergel blurted.

'Exactly...' Cal replied. 'Our visitors had sent their probe here to leave the beacon...a marker...for future use. Jess, what did Professor Walker have to tell us about the exact location of the coordinates?'

Jess returned to her laptop and changed the projection on the screen to a map of Ireland and the British Isles. 'Well, he said that location is in a body of water, namely the Atlantic Ocean.' She zoomed in on the location. 'But, he said that it does have some history. He stated that ancient maps actually depict an island in that exact location. Most historians believe that the island is nothing more than lore, but the maps do show it as existing...at some points...and cartographers are not known to simply forge maps. There are also some people in history that actually stated that they visited the island. The island is known as Hy Brasil.'

Cal grunted. 'Hmmm...I've heard of it, but let's see what an internet search brings up on that...Jess?'

Jess typed the name into her computer and then projected a history on screen.

Professor Hogan silently entered the room and took a seat.

'So, they are looking for this...Hy Brasil, but it doesn't exist.' Breyer blurted.

Cal moved towards the screen. 'It doesn't exist currently, but it may have in the past. Look, they stated that they followed their probe. The craft witnessed by the Air Force in 1980 was smallish...not large enough to hold "beings" of any sort...thus, in my opinion, it was a probe. That probe was searching for Hy Brasil...it gave the coordinates to the military, as though it was asking for directions.'

'The island wasn't there in 1980 either.' Olivia said.

'No, it wasn't.' Cal replied. 'The probe couldn't locate it...it appears...and was searching for it through other means...maybe flying around the near vicinity to recalibrate like a GPS system or something... or was actually looking for someone to give it directions. It did pass the coordinates on to the military personnel. When it had no success it went to the closest land-based location to the where the island was supposed to have been. That location was here...' He pointed to the screen. 'The furthest southwestern coast of Ireland.' He stood stoically before them. 'My opinion is that the probe was to leave a beacon on the island to later be followed, at some point in time, by the...alien race that created it. When it couldn't locate the island it left the beacon in the closest location. That beacon is the rock that we have in the other room. When our visitors came to find the beacon it wasn't near the location it was intended, since our antiquities dealer had picked it up and brought it with him to the United States.'

'Our rock *is* a beacon...and that's why it glows when they're near by?' Jess said with hands on either cheek.

Cal nodded. 'Yes, and they've been following it and finally arrived. It appears, from their need to follow the Pioneer craft's directions to earth, that when the beacon was moved it didn't operate correctly.'

'Holy crap!' Jergel said. 'That rock is from some distant planet?'

'It appears so, Jergs.' Cal said.

'Far out!' Jergel replied with a smile.

Professor Hogan, who had silently listened to most of the discussion, addressed the group. 'Yes, far out, Jergel. I want to thank all of you for the updates and analysis. You are an excellent group. This is something that is truly incredible and...I must implore you not to discuss these findings or theories with anyone. We need to be on top of this and not let it get away from us. Understood?'

The group nodded.

'Now, I have a question. If there were coordinates in the first message... were there any in the ones received in last night's message?'

Cal shrugged. 'We haven't checked that yet...good point.'

Olivia moved to her computer. 'I'll check that now. I can access the program from here…shouldn't take more than a few minutes. When it comes up I'll put it on the screen.'

The group discussed the findings amongst themselves and then heard Olivia emphatically hitting the keys on her computer keyboard.

'I have something.' She said. 'There are actually two coordinates appearing, but in South America.'

'Let's see it, Liv.' Cal said pointing to the screen.

A map of South America soon appeared on the screen and then the coordinates narrowed the location to the country of Peru.

'Peru?' Professor Hogan said while staring at the screen.

'Two locations in Peru.' Olivia replied as she used a laser pointer to pinpoint the locations. 'Here…and here.'

'Let's zoom in on those, Liv.' Cal said standing next to the screen. 'Then let's get a satellite view.'

Olivia returned to the computer and made the adjustments and both locations soon were visible.

'Oh…wow!' Jess exclaimed.

'That's unbelievable!' Cal said. 'The Nazca Lines and the Band of Holes.'

'What does that mean, Cal? How are they significant?' Jess asked.

He walked closer towards the screen. 'Both of these locations are known to be great mysteries in many circles…archaeological and otherwise. These locations have been dated to ancient times, yet were not discovered until the 20th century…even though they were in plain sight. It wasn't until man developed the ability of flight were they first noticed. Basically, they are primarily visible and significant only from the air.'

'Dude,' Jergel chimed in. 'If they are from ancient times, those people couldn't fly planes to see them. Why would you make something…as large as that…and not even be able to see them?'

'Exactly.' Cal replied. 'They are known as geoglyphs. The theory that many have is that they were created for others…who could fly.'

'Huh?' Olivia said with a quizzical look. 'Who could fly in ancient times other than…?'

Cal nodded and looked at each of them individually. 'Yes, who else? The Nazca Lines are graphic depictions of figures…enormous in size…some are 600 feet across. One of the figures has been called the "Spaceman" or "Astronaut", since he appears to be wearing a space helmet. There are also many long, straight, lines, hence the name Nazca Lines…that appear and have been theorized to be aviation runways. The Band of Holes…also in Peru…is a line of holes dug into the earth in a pattern that goes on for miles. Some believe that they exist for viewing from above also and the two locations are tied together.'

'Aviation runways?' Breyer said. 'In an era where airplanes were not even remotely imaginable?'

'Yes,' Cal replied. 'And now our visitors are…referencing them.'

Chapter 13

Former President Jimmy Carter openly admits that he witnessed an Unidentified Flying Object (UFO) around 7:30 PM in October 1969, while waiting outside for Lion's Club meeting in Leary, Georgia. Carter and twelve others witnesses saw a "Very bright object with changing colors and about the size of the moon. The object hovered 30 degrees above the horizon and moved towards the Earth and then away, before disappearing into the distance." In 1973, Carter filed an official report of the sighting with the National Investigations Committee on Aerial Phenomena (NICAP).

The following day, Cal and Jess met at the coffee shop prior to their shift. There they discussed their plan of action in regards to approaching the university to receive permission to attempt communication with the "visitors."

'I think that we have enough to go on, Jess, I really do. It's almost to the point where it can't be ignored.' Cal said.

'I know…I know.' She answered. 'I'm just a little hesitant. I know Professor Hogan and the others will back us up, but the president…not sure about him. He will take the high-road, if necessary.'

Cal nodded. 'Yes, but he doesn't have much of an option. This is huge.'

'We have to do it professionally, Cal…very professional. A well-planned presentation, etc.' She said between sips of her coffee.

'It will be good, believe me.' He replied. 'We'll have Olivia, Jergel, and Breyer all give their spiel, as well as some of the professors who provided us with information. Hang on…here's a text from Breyer.'

'What the hell?' He exclaimed staring at his phone.

'What is it?' Jess asked.

'You've got to be….Breyer says that the military came to the observatory this morning. They questioned Professor Hogan for four hours. He says that the observatory is on lock down until further notice!'

'What? They can't do that!' Jess exclaimed.

'Well, they did. They are trying to quash this whole thing! We need to get in touch with Professor Hogan to see what is really going on.' He said.

'What are we going to do? We can't even go in for our shift tonight.' She answered.

'Hey, I have the keys to the observatory's truck…it has the mobile equipment. There should be enough equipment in there to give us a chance to keep the project going. We can't let them stop this now, we're in too deep. The problem is the van is parked behind of the observatory.

We'll have to scope it out to see if they are blocking access to that area. Let's head out…I know where we can get a good view.'

Cal drove his SUV, while Jess rode shotgun working her phone. She was attempting to call Professor Hogan and sending texts to some of the others. Professor Hogan didn't answer and she followed with a text also. 'Hey, Breyer said not to attempt to go through the main entrance… they have it blocked. He's not sure of the rear entrance, but he assumes it will be too.' She said.

'They'll have them both blocked.' Cal replied. 'We'll head over to the hillside overlooking the observatory from the East. We should be able to get a good view of what's happening from there.'

'Oh, wow!' Jess exclaimed. 'Believe it or not…Jergel says he has the "moon" rock. He took it on his way out.'

'Great…that was brilliant! That thing freaks him out, so I know it wasn't easy for him to do that.' Cal said taking both hands off of the steering wheel and holding them high in the air.

'How are we going to get the van out if both entrances are blocked?' Jess asked.

Cal looked over at her and winked. Jess, caught off guard, felt flushed by the move. She turned and stared out of the windshield not to reveal that both sides of her cheeks were pink.

'Are you okay?' Cal asked with a smirk. He had obviously noticed her reaction.

'Yes! It's just a little hot in here.' She said while slightly rolling down the window.

At 6:00 PM, they arrived at the bottom of a grass-covered hill, which was an approximately five hundred yards from the observatory. They slowly climbed the hill, using a few bushes and trees as cover. They reached the summit and hunched down between two shrubs, which sat beneath a large oak tree. Cal took out his binoculars and peered towards the observatory. He scanned left, right, and left again.

'Both entrances are blocked, but lightly. There are two guards at the main gate and one at the back.' Cal said still peering. 'There are three other cars in front of the building. None of them belong to the employees.'

'So, what's the plan, big boy?' Jess said with a smile.

'Big boy always has a plan...honey.' He returned the smile. 'Do you remember the old maintenance road?'

'The maintenance road? Yes, they only use that when they have to move something very large because it has direct access to the loading area.'

'Exactly.' Cal answered returning to the binoculars. 'From what I see... it's not being monitored and the mobile observatory unit...the truck... is to the right of the loading dock.'

'Huh? What do you suggest?' Jess answered.

Cal hung the binoculars around his neck. 'Well, my plan is to get the truck...I have the keys. I will get to the observatory from the maintenance road and drive the truck right out of there through that road. You can cover me from up here...text me if you see movement in that direction.'

'Isn't there a gate at the entrance to that road? How are you going to get the truck through?' Jess said.

'Yes, but I will find my way around it. It only blocks the center of the road. Once I'm through, I will meet up with you here...you take my SUV and we'll rendezvous just outside of the university. While I'm on my way to the truck, you can text the rest of the crew to meet us at the cathedral.'

'Got it...' She said nodding.

'Okay...I'm heading out...starting to get dark.' Cal replied.

'Hey...' She said. 'Be careful...big boy.'

'Got it...' He smiled.

Cal found his way back down the hill and cautiously moved along the perimeter towards the observatory. He slid into a small valley that contained a slow moving creek. He followed the creek for several hundred yards and spotted the entrance to the gravel maintenance road, which did have a basic swing-out gate chained at the center. The maintenance road was off of small side roads, which lead to the main road. He texted Jess and asked if she noticed any movement. The reply was that no one had moved from their position. Cal immediately headed past the gate, which was wooded on both sides. He slowly followed the short road from the wooded area and reached the end point where it led onto the observatory grounds. Still in the wooded area, he checked his pockets for the van keys and texted Jess for clearance. She replied that there was still no movement.

Cal spotted the truck and decided to slowly walk towards it. He knew he would reach a point where the guard at the rear entrance could see him, but he had no choice. He could only hope that he wouldn't be spotted in the brief window. As the evening dusk crawled in, he walked into the clearing and towards the truck. He checked his phone for messages from Jess, but none were received. He spotted the guard at the back gate and he wasn't facing in his direction, so he picked up his pace. He surmised that he wasn't noticed and slightly trotted towards the truck with keys in hand. He reached the truck, unlocked the door and jumped inside, but didn't close the door. He looked in the direction of the guard station, which was out view and didn't notice any movement. He checked his phone again...no messages from Jess.

Cal slowly and lightly closed the door of the truck. He placed the keys in the ignition, knowing that the engine sound could be heard at the back gate, if not the front gate also. He turned the key and the engine fired beautifully. He put the truck in reverse and turned it quickly towards the maintenance road. He immediately heard his phone buzz and vibrate with a text message. He looked quickly at the message and it was from Jess. He opened it and all that it said was...*MOVE!'*

As he reached the maintenance road, he laid into the gas pedal and gravel spewed for several yards. The gravel road was not routinely maintained and contained a number of dips and holes, which rocked the truck at this speed. He evaded those that he could and headed for the gate. He could barely see flashing lights in his rear view mirror, but knew he was being followed. He had traveled this road several times in the past and was aware that the left side of the gate contained nothing more than high grass and weeds. He headed directly for that area, picked up speed and held on. He barreled through the vegetation, which did not have a further barrier. The large truck slide sideways and onto the side road for several yards until Cal regained control and straightened it out. He stopped for a second and then sped down the road. He knew he would have a minute or two to spare, since his followers would be perplexed by the vans ability to get through the gate without opening it. He would use the extra time to meet up with Jess and get onto the main road. Several minutes later, he saw Jess in his SUV and sped past her, waving her on. She was immediately on his tail and they reached the main road without incident, though signs of sirens were slightly heard in the distance.

CHAPTER 14

Former President Ronald Reagan is known to have had two UFO sightings. While Governor of California, Reagan and his wife Nancy were late for a Hollywood dinner party on the California coast. Upon their arrival, the Reagans were disturbed and excited. They claimed that they were late due to a UFO sighting that they had stopped to watch. The Reagan account was often coborated by stars Lucille Ball and Steve Allen, who were at the party.

In 1974, Governor Reagan was traveling in a small plane with security personnel and a pilot. At 10:00 PM, the plane encountered a UFO. Per Reagan's account shortly after the incident: "I was in a plane last week and I looked out of the window and saw this white light. It was zigzagging around, so I went up to the pilot and asked if he had seen anything like that before? The pilot replied "Nope! But let's follow it." We followed it for several minutes. It was a bright white light. We followed it to Bakersfield and all of a sudden, to our utter amazement, it went straight up into the heavens." The pilot backed Reagan's version of the UFO sighting and stated that they had discussed it throughout the years.

Approaching the university, Cal parked the truck on a tree-lined street near the bustling campus. He patiently waited several minutes and then began to place a call to Jess. Just as he was about to place the call, she pulled in behind him. Jess slowly exited his SUV and entered the truck's passenger door. She wore a worried, but wide smile. 'That was pretty impressive.' She said. Cal nodded and smiled. 'Shouldn't have come to this, but it needed to be done. I don't think that they followed us far, but they know it's a university vehicle and may come looking for it here.'

'Yeah, but I think that we're fine on this street…sort of secluded.' She replied looking out of the window.

'You're probably right, but we'll hide the truck a little more and then walk to the cathedral. Are the others on their way?'

Jess pulled out her phone. 'It looks like they can make it…they should be there within the half-hour.'

'Great.' Cal answered while starting the engine. 'Let's see if Paolo will let us park this mobile unit behind his pizza shop.' The truck pulled out and headed for a nearby side street. After purchasing a few slices of pizza and drinks to go, Paolo readily agreed to allow the truck to be parked behind his building. As they cautiously walked to the cathedral, Cal and Jess indulged in their pizza.

They asked the others to meet them in a spare room just inside a secondary entrance. Upon entering, they were greeted by Bob Breyer who was busily replying to messages on his phone. Several minutes later, Olivia and Jergel also made their way to the specified location.

'Okay…it looks like we're all here.' Cal said addressing the group and he immediately updated them on what had occurred at the observatory and how they came to meet in this room.

'What I plan to do now is to bring the mobile observatory unit to the rural area, north of the city, where we've determined that our visitors have been stopping in the sky and making contact with us from that specific coordinate. Once there, we'll use the mobile equipment to attempt contact.'

'Dude, what kind of contact are you talking about?' Jergel asked while nervously scratching his head.

'Well…we're hoping that they find us there…primarily due to the moon rock. Thanks again for taking that, Jergs…I'm convinced it's the beacon that they're following.'

'No problem, Dude…I mean, I know it's a key to this whole thing in some way.'

'So, outside of that,' Cal continued. 'We've asked Liv and Bob to convert the algorithms into a message that "they" will understand. Basically, we'll use the system that they've used to communicate with us, but, this time, we'll be contacting them.'

'I think we can do it.' Breyer replied. 'We've been feeding their messages into the program and we have developed a ballpark system of the numerically related alphabet. With that, we should be able to draft a message.'

'All we need to know, Cal, is what that message is to say.' Olivia said, radiantly dressed as usual.

Cal smiled. 'Yes, that is the question. Well, they are here for a reason…a need of some sort. They are searching for a location where this beacon… the rock…is supposed to lead them. We know where that location is. The message will be…*We can help you.*'

'We also plan to send them the coordinates to the location off of the coast of Ireland…where the rock was supposedly to be.' Jess interjected. 'The location of the mysterious island of Hy Brasil.'

'The island doesn't exist, Jess.' Jergel said. 'That's what the professor said.'

'It appeared on ancient maps at one time.' Cal replied. 'Islands just don't disappear…it's now below the water line.'

'My interpretation is that they are in need of some natural resource that existed on that island.' Breyer said. 'You're right, Bob,' Cal said slightly pacing the room. 'Do you remember the Nazca Lines in Peru that they projected to us? They were here before and the natives, the Nazca people, created those 70 enormous drawings and 300 geometric figures specifically for them, as well as the 800 straight lines or…landing strips. Now, do you recall the Band of Holes in Peru that they also depicted? In archaeological circles, the primary explanation is that the holes were lit with fire – as a beacon that could easily be seen from above. In other circles, they believe that the holes were attempts at extracting minerals…natural resources of some type. The Nazca area is known to contain very high levels of Nitrates. We're all scientists here…and we know that Nitrates are used in rocket fuel. The theory is that the mineral extraction was the primary purpose…then, once the minerals were exhausted…they left.'

'And the natives then lit the holes with fire in an attempt at attracting them back.' Jess said.

'Exactly…' Cal nodded. 'My theory is that they found another location for the same or another needed material, which was Hy Brasil.'

The room was silent for a few moments.

'Plausible…' Breyer finally blurted. 'It's certainly plausible. So, we're going to provide them with the coordinates of Hy Brasil…via a numerical code?'

'Yes, that's the plan.' Cal replied looking directly at him. Breyer nodded and looked over to Olivia who also nodded in agreement.

'Okay, we're set then. Jess and I will drive the truck to the rural location northeast of I-79. Jergs, you follow us in my SUV…I have a few more pieces of equipment in there we can use. Oh…and bring the rock. Bob… Liv…use the university computer labs and draft up the message. Then meet us at the location…call us if you can't find it.'

CHAPTER 15

In 2017, NASA will launch the transiting Exoplanet
Surveying Satellite – in a search for alien planets and life.

North of the city, the mobile observatory unit trekked along the interstate with Cal keeping an eye on Jergel following them in his SUV. A little more than forty-five minutes later the GPS coordinate approached. The truck exited the highway and traversed several side roads into increasingly rural territory. Farms were visible on either side of the road, each having cattle and horses and with an occasional herd of sheep. They knew that they couldn't risk setting up their equipment on private land and made the decision to find a location in the closest public park, which they did rather easily.

Once they were within the park, they pulled the vehicles off of the main road and stopped near a shelter. The light of day was already escaping and the team decided to move the vehicles more so into an open field nearby. Parking the vehicles, they began to set up the highly sophisticated mobile astronomy lab, which was basically the back of the large truck. The roof of the unit opened, allowing two powerful telescopes to peer through. A smaller, third telescope was set-up outside. Jess sat at one of two workstations in the unit's compartment and she worked to start the computer systems and radar, ensuring that they synced with the computers at the university and the observatory. They disabled their GPS location on the systems and their phones so that their location could not be determined.

'Hey,' Jergs said as he stood by the open back door of the truck. 'Dude, this truck smells like pizza...where is it? I'm hungry.'

'You must be,' Cal said. 'I saw you eyeing up some old hotdogs left on the grill back at the shelter. We had the unit parked behind Paolo's... that's why it smells so good. There are some snacks in the cabinet in the corner...help yourself.'

'All systems are coming up to full strength, Cal. We should be good to go soon.' Jess said as she wore a pair of headphones.

'Good. Jergs…text Breyer and see how they are coming.' Cal said to Jergel who was digging through the snack cabinet. Jergel nodded between bites of a granola bar.

Cal sat down at the other workstation and moved the two telescopes into position. He then rolled his chair to one and peered through. He followed the maneuver with the second scope also. He then returned to the control panel and slid two levers that raised large antennae on the truck's roof.

'They've written the code and have emailed it to you, Dude. They're on their way and should be here shortly.' Jergel said to Cal.

'Okay…this is going well. Jergs, please set-up the outside scope to a north/north east position. Check the radar dish too.' Cal said while working his panel.

'Got it…' Jergel replied as he headed out of the rear door of the unit.

Cal logged into his computer and accessed his email account. Sure enough, the email from Olivia had been received. Upon opening it, it was nothing more than a long string of numbers, a numerical code, primarily of the numbers zero and one. He was hoping that it was correct and that they provided the coordinates of Hy Brasil and the statement…*We can help you.*'

'How are we proposing to get the message to our visitors, Cal?' Jess asked after she noticed he had the code. 'I mean, they have the technology to project their statements onto our screens, but how are we to do it for them?'

Cal sat back in his chair and sighed. 'We attract them with the beacon, which we'll place in the middle of this field. Once they arrive, they will notice us, as usual. They always scan our computer systems before they make contact. We'll make certain that the only item on our screens is the code. They will immediately recognize a code system that they have used and I'm sure that they will read it. I know that it's a shot in the dark...no pun intended...but, it's a chance at history.'

Fifteen minutes later, a vehicle could be seen approaching their position from the rear. Cal and Jergel pulled binoculars to view it. After a few seconds, it was apparent that it was Breyer's SUV and he pulled the vehicle behind the other two. Breyer and Olivia exited and headed for the mobile unit. They joined the others in the back where Cal informed them of his plan to provide the code to the visitors. Jergel retrieved the rock from the back of Cal's SUV and carried it approximately fifty yards from their position. He nestled it into the ground and walked back. He then sat in Cal's SUV and worked a pair of binoculars. His function was to listen to chatter on the radio band dedicated to military police, via a scanner. If he heard anything interesting he was to inform the group and he was to watch for approaching vehicles. Breyer pulled up a chair and manned the external telescope. Cal and Jess each handled the unit's telescopes, while Olivia sat at one of the truck's workstations and handled the computer communications.

'Testing...testing...' Cal said into his headset. 'Everyone on-board?'

They replied, one at a time that they were all in position.

'Hey, Cal,' Jergel chimed in. 'I bet NASA had better headsets than these, Dude. Neil Armstrong wouldn't have put up with these.'

'They work, Jergs...that's all that matters.' Cal replied.

'Speaking of my man, Neil,' Jergel continued. 'Tell me, Dude, is the Mr. Gorsky story true?

'What's the Mr. Gorsky story?' Olivia asked.

'Funny as hell it is...come on, Cal...what's the scoop?' Jergel laughed.

'We're kind of busy right now, Jergs, but...to cut the tension, tell them the story.' Cal answered in a distracted tone.

'Oh, wow...you people don't know it?' He replied. 'You see, when Neil A. was a kid he and his friends were playing baseball in Neil's yard. The one Dude hits the ball pretty far and it lands under Neil's neighbor's window...which was open. Neil runs out to pick up the ball and he hears an argument between his neighbors...the Gorskys. Seems like Mr. Gorsky wants some "action"...if you know what I mean...trying to keep it clean...from Mrs. Gorsky and she isn't having any of it. She tells Mr. Gorsky..."Yeah, you'll get some...you'll get some alright...when the neighbor kid lands on the moon...that's when you'll get it." Jergel laughs loudly. 'Neil A. heard this. So, when Neil A. lands on the moon he says..."Good luck, Mr. Gorsky!" He laughs uncontrollably as does everyone else.

'Really, Cal...is that story true?' Olivia asks.

'Pure hearsay...' Cal replies.

'Come on, Dude...NASA has you sworn you to secrecy or something. You know it's true.' Jergel chuckled.

'Only Neil would know for sure. Any chatter from the military radio band, Jergs?' He asked.

'Dude, they have an APB out on the truck, but it appears that they have no clue where it's at.' He replied.

'Let's keep it that way. Turning on scopes...let's stay on the radar, Liv. Let us know if you see an anomaly moving towards the beacon.' Cal said into his headset.

'This is Bob; I have the outside scope locked onto the exact coordinates that the object has appeared in the past. As a side-note, I wonder what the Air Force is doing to my files in the observatory? I mean, it bothers me...' Breyer snorted.

'I'm sure it does...I'm sure it does.' Cal answered softly. 'They want to know what we know, but the files are so encrypted that it will take them weeks to break into them.'

'Why can't they see the object, Cal? Or anyone else for that matter?' Olivia chimed in.

'Haven't anyone of you watched *Star Trek*? Our visitors are very advanced, obviously, or they wouldn't even be able to travel to Earth. They are cloaking themselves...not allowing themselves to be seen...except to those who hold their beacon. Simple.'

'Yeah, simple, big boy.' Jess chuckled.

Olivia cleared her throat. 'So, you're saying that they are only allowing themselves to be seen by those...who they want to be seen by?'

'You got it, Liv. *Star Trek* technology in the first degree.' Cal replied as he stared through the scope.

'Well, I have some action on our technology...' Olivia replied. 'Anomaly appearing on the radar screen...high-speed object traveling west to east.'

'Everyone in position...' Cal answered as he swung the scope in the direction. 'Is it in the northern sky?'

'Yes, it appears so.' Liv said as she adjusted her screen.

'I'm picking something up faintly.' Breyer answered.

Jess moved her scope also. 'I should be able to lock onto it in a few seconds.' She said.

'I'm onto it.' Cal replied. 'It's coming in our direction. Jergs...put the binoculars onto the moon rock.'

'Okay, Dude. Getting pretty dark...hope I can see it.' He answered.

'If it works the way it's supposed to...shouldn't be a problem.' Cal said sarcastically. 'Is it glowing?'

'Yeah, Dude...like the fourth of July.' Jergel said.

'I've got a clear visual.' Breyer uttered. 'Incredible...should be above us in approximately ten minutes.'

'Confirmed.' Jess replied. 'Definitely the same type of craft we observed from the observatory. They're probably intrigued by the new location of the beacon.'

'Yes, especially since it's near their normal coordinates. It should be very alluring to them.' Cal said while peering through his scope.

Jergel laughed loudly. 'Dude, even aliens are curious.'

Cal turned from the telescope. 'Liv, clear the two computer screens of all information and data.'

'Will do...' She answered while working her keyboards.

'Once they're clear...upload the message onto the screens.' Cal continued. 'Leave the message on the screens until they depart.'

'Messages loading onto both screens now.' Olivia said. 'Radar indicates that the object will be above us soon.'

'Okay...all scopes lock onto the known coordinate.' Cal ordered. 'We need to monitor the situation...plus, we'll get a hell of view from here.'

Breyer grunted. 'Cal, what's the danger quota? I mean, should we be worried? Did you learn anything about this at NASA?'

'My guess is minimal...but, that is a hypothesis.' Cal replied. 'They have shown no aggressive behavior. You're between the vehicles right now, Bob. If you feel that you are in any danger, get inside of one of them.'

'Will do, Mr. NASA. I'm good right now. I wonder what they eat? Pasta?' He answered.

Within minutes the large triangular-shaped craft silently slipped into the sky above them, well before it was anticipated. The object depicted three lights at each corner that slowly pulsated in bright white and an opaque shade of yellow. It hovered some two hundred yards directly above the rock beacon, which glowed brighter than ever before. Surprisingly, no sound was emitted by the craft and the bright lights surprisingly did not reflect off of the ground below.

'Oh, man! Dude, this is freaking me out!' Jergel blurted. 'This is freaking me out! I wasn't worried before, but now....it's huge!'

'Hold your ground, Jergs.' Cal answered softly. 'No need to panic.'

'Just incredible...incredible!' Breyer chimed in. 'I can't believe it...just can't.'

Cal chuckled. 'I'm just glad that all of you can now corroborate our story. Liv, go and have a look through the windshield.'

'Thought that you'd never ask.' She darted from her seat towards the truck's cabin. 'Oh, wow! I'm in total awe! This is mind blowing, guys.' She uttered. 'Look! It's shining a light down towards the beacon!'

Cal grabbed his binoculars and moved towards the windshield. 'Good show…now, finish that scan and move towards our computers.' He said moving back to his scope and focused his scope directly at the front of the craft. He could discern an odd, shiny, metallic exterior with small lettering or graphics to the right side, which appeared to be written in a hieroglyphic style. He raised his scope towards the supposed cockpit area and noticed a frosted glass type material approximately five feet across. From behind the glass came a glow that he had never seen before, and within it, veiled forms stood. No more could be determined.

'I can see the odd exterior with graphics and a type of a window.' He said a little out of breath.

'Can you see inside the window, Cal?' Jess asked. 'I can't get a focus from my position.'

'Yes…I can to an extent. *Something…something…*is in there. Can't see well, but, *yes*.' He answered.

A minute later, the craft's downward light moved steadily from the rock and towards the vehicles. Breyer jumped into his SUV. The light pierced the interior of the truck and moved stealthy through the equipment. Upon reaching the computers, it paused for several seconds and then moved on. It then moved to the other two vehicles, causing a panic of the occupants. The light quickly retracted into the craft.

'This actually may work.' Cal said. 'It… may actually work. Hold your positions and let's see what happens.'

The scene was silent for several minutes. Cal and Jess locked the telescopes onto the craft, which still hovered above the beacon. Olivia logged back into the computers and checked the radar, while Jergel and Breyer used binoculars to monitor the situation from within their respective vehicles. 'Too quiet, Dude…just a little too quiet.' Jergel said. 'Wait…something just came across the scanner.'

'What do you have, Jergs?' Cal asked.

'Sounds like the military police are heading north…they're not saying where they're heading, but they're on the interstate.' He replied.

Cal grunted. 'Keep us updated. We can assume they're heading in our direction…even though we covered our tracks. Everyone make sure your GPS systems on your gadgets are off. Let's start the engines on these vehicles so that we can head out if we need too.'

'Roger that. Jergs, let's get the equipment outside and put it in the back of these vehicles.' Breyer replied and the sound of his SUV starting filled the microphone on their headsets.

Cal moved to the driver's seat of the truck and fired up the engine. He looked up through the windshield and was in awe of the magnificent craft that stood out like a star against the dark sky. He heard an exclamation from the back of the truck and returned to his seat. 'What's up, Liv?'

'They are projecting something on our screens again…it's the depiction of the Pioneer message. The nude human figures…male and female.' She replied adjusting the screen size for a close-up.

Cal and Jess both moved towards the screens.

'Actually…' Liv started. 'These humans look familiar for some reason.'

Cal and Jess moved closer to the screen for even a better view. Cal picked up the scent of Jess' perfume as his face moved closer to hers. The faces on the screen were definitely familiar, especially to them.

'Hey! These faces are familiar because it's your face and Jess'!' Olivia said in astonishment.

Jess smiled widely and laughed softly. 'Yes…they are. I can say for a fact that our faces weren't on the originals that were sent into space years ago.'

'You weren't even born then, girlfriend.' Olivia replied with a chuckle. 'I think they are trying to tell you something.'

Cal sighed. 'Yes…it's us. I think I'm a little better looking than that, but I'll take it.'

Jess smacked his arm. 'Yeah, looks like me, but I'd kill for a body like that.' She said with a laugh.

Cal turned to her. Their faces were within inches of each other as they viewed the screen. They looked into each others eyes and both smiled softly. 'Actually,' Cal replied. 'I kind of think that yours is better.'

Jess smiled wider. 'Really? Well, big boy…thanks.'

Cal held back an impulse to kiss her. Even with an alien craft hovering above them, military police on their way to their location and Olivia sitting next to them…he wanted to. The urge at this moment said something to him about Jess.

Their moment was broken by Jergel's voice coming through the headsets. 'Hey Dudes…and Dudettes…sorry…sounds like the MPs are getting close to the exit off of the interstate.'

'Thanks, Jergs.' Cal replied and slowly moved back to his seat, but without taking his gaze away from Jess.

'I'm seeing some movement from the craft on the radar.' Olivia chimed in. Cal moved to the cabin of the truck, while Jess moved back to her telescope.

'They're moving!' Breyer said excitedly. 'And the beacon is gone.'

Within seconds, the craft slipped higher into the sky and was out of visual sight. Cal walked back to the rear of the truck and began to bring down the scopes.

'Liv, see if you can follow them on the radar. We're heading out everyone… let's go.' He said.

CHAPTER 16

"There may be aliens in our Milky Way galaxy and there are billions of other galaxies. The probability is almost CERTAIN that there is life somewhere in space." Apollo 11 astronaut.

A short while later, the three-vehicle caravan was traveling south on the interstate and heading for the university. Bob Breyer was in the lead vehicle and Jergel brought up the rear. With their mission basically accomplished, the crew didn't fear the aspect of heading for the university, but they had no intention of returning to the observatory.

Cal drove the mobile observatory truck with Jess and Olivia still working on tracking the craft from the radar.

'What do you have for me, ladies?' Cal asked through his headset.

'They are heading east...they're over the Atlantic right now.' Jess replied.

'That's what I was hoping for.' Cal answered. 'They are heading in the direction of the coordinates of Hy Brasil...which we provided to them. Let me know when they stop.'

'Roger that.' Jess said. 'We are also picking up some feeds from other observatories, Cal. They are tracking something.'

'The craft? That can't be...they've been cloaked to everyone but us up until now.' He said while slightly turning his head towards the rear of the truck.

'No...No. It's a celestial object of some nature. I'm seeing chatter about it coming into Earth's atmosphere within four hours.' Jess said in a worried tone. 'I wish we could get back to the observatory...our capabilities are limited in this mobile unit.'

'Bob...Jergs...you heard that. Scan your radio stations to see if the news is saying anything too.'

'Okay...will do.' Both replied.

'Jess, that can only be an asteroid of some kind. There are no known celestial objects scheduled to enter the atmosphere...what are you hearing?' Cal asked.

Jess grunted. 'Yes, you're right. It appeared in views several hours ago... totally unexpected...just like the one in Russia a few years back. The problem is that current projections have it possibly striking the planet.

It's fairly large and could cause some problems, but all of the information and data they have on it is sketchy.'

'I just received a text from Professor Hogan.' Breyer said. 'He wants to know where we're at and if we're aware of this object? He's home and listening to the chatter too.'

'Don't read your texts while you're driving, Bob.' Olivia replied. 'We have a pending disaster on our hands already.'

'Will do...' He replied.

'I'm hearing a couple of things on the military band,' Jergel said. 'It looks like they are calling the MPs back to the base...for what they're calling, *pending disaster readiness*. The MPs that were on their way to our location are heading back south on the interstate...they could be behind us soon.'

'Let's get off at the upcoming rest stop...we don't need any aggravation right now.' Cal replied. 'We'll watch them go by and then get back onto the highway. Bob, when we get there, reply to Professor Hogan and ask him to meet us at the university. See if he can secure the same room that we met in earlier.'

The three vehicles soon pulled into the rest stop and they took their turns using the facilities and grabbing a needed beverage or snack. As they sat watching the interstate, they soon noticed two military vehicles drive past their location and continuing south. A few minutes later, the caravan made its way back onto the highway and headed in the same direction.

The caravan made it to the cathedral without incident and Cal pulled the truck near the secondary door that they had entered several hours ago. The truck was flanked by the two SUVs and a fourth car was that of Professor Hogan. Cal and Breyer entered the spare room and found the Professor working at a laptop. He greeted them enthusiastically.

'Good to see you,' He said. 'You had me worried.'

'We're all good, Professor.' Cal said. 'What are you hearing?'

'Looks like it's an unknown and unexpected asteroid entering the atmosphere, Cal. Still not a lot of details, but it may strike in the Atlantic Ocean near the equator...even within a few hours.' He replied with a serious tone.

'Must be moving much faster than we initially heard. That would cause some serious problems.' Cal said as he took a seat. 'Tidal waves... tsunamis...not a good situation.'

'It could be far reaching, Cal.' The professor said. 'I think that we'd be fairly safe as far inland as we are, but the waterways, including those here, would be affected.'

'Yeah, it would depend upon how large of an asteroid it is.' Breyer said, while also taking a seat.

As they contemplated the situation, Jess burst into the room. 'Hey....the craft has stopped. It is above the coordinates for Hy Brasil.'

A slight smile crossed Cal's face and even those of the others. 'At least there is some good news. They should be able to access their needed resources...and return home. Though, I'm sure that they are aware of the asteroid also. Considering that they are above the Atlantic too...it will be interesting to see their reaction to such an object.'

Everyone nodded. 'Jess, keep us updated on their movements. Tell Jergel to continue to scan for news of the asteroid from the national news sources also.' The professor said. 'I would love to go back to the observatory, but the military is still there from what I hear. We may be able to help with the object tracking from there.'

'I think that they've given up the chase on us right now...more important things to worry about, I guess.' Cal said as he scanned his phone for news of the asteroid. 'We can use the mobile unit as much as possible, Professor. We'll get back in there in a few minutes.'

The door opened and Jergel came in. 'Dude, Liv said for everyone to come to the truck. Something about the asteroid showing up on the screens.'

The group exited the room and entered the rear door of the mobile unit. Both Olivia and Jess were working feverously at the two workstations.

'We have the asteroid on the radar screen...it is closer than expected.' Olivia said.

Breyer raised the mobile unit scopes and he and the Professor manned one each.

'We should be getting live shots from some sources soon.' Jess said. 'Jergs...put the national news on the televisions.'

Jergel flicked on two small-screen TVs situated in the upper corners of the unit. He also accessed a laptop for the same purpose.

'There will be panic in the streets soon.' The professor said. 'Maybe even more than if they knew an alien craft is over the Atlantic as we speak.'

Cal sighed loudly as he worked a computer. 'Yes, it's ironic that there is something that would cause hysteria more than a known alien craft on Earth. Let's take that as a sign...they are not our greatest fear and we should take that into consideration.'

'Hey, everyone, take a moment and contact your family and friends.' The professor said. 'Tell them the situation and just to take shelter... especially if they live nearby or inland. If they live near the ocean fronts... tell them to move as inland as possible.'

'What's the situation with the craft, Jess...Liv?' Cal asked.

'Still in the same position...it has made slight movements westward, but that's about it.' Jess replied as she analyzed the screen.

'Hey, Dudes, it does look like people are panicking across the world. National news is reporting that there is utter chaos in some cities, especially near the ocean fronts.' Jergel said. 'I looked outside and there are even a number of people running across the campus here.'

Professor Hogan pulled his phone from his sport coat. 'The university president just texted me...wants to know what the situation is? I'll tell him what we know, which isn't much.'

'I'm getting an ever so slight visual of something approaching from the western sky.' Breyer said as he peered through the telescope. 'Has to be the asteroid...'

'When the news feeds pick it up the panic will go over-the-top.' Cal said. 'There is really nothing that can be done at this point. We have been developing technology to counteract such a strike, but we are no way ready to put it into action.' He paused and reflected on the comet that passed by the Earth on the night that the observatory dome malfunctioned. He yearned for an asteroid appearance of only that magnitude.

Olivia gave out a whimper. 'Reports have the object striking within the hour...it is moving far faster than anticipated.'

'They are saying in the same location, Liv.' Jergel blurted as he stated at the TV screen. 'Atlantic Ocean...near the equator.'

'Okay, everyone, all we can do is monitor the situation.' The Professor said. 'Scopes, radar and news sources...keep everyone updated on what you see and hear.'

The room went quiet for several minutes as everyone performed their duties, but with worried anticipation of what may occur. Cal's curiosity of the craft's reaction to the approaching asteroid led him to monitor their location at the same time.

'Hey, the craft is moving!' He said excitedly. 'Slight westward movement and gaining altitude.'

'Are they leaving?' Jess asked.

'The location they were in, yes, but they are still in the atmosphere at this point.' Cal replied. 'Though...they are entering sub-space now.'

'They're getting the hell out of here....' The Professor murmured. 'They have what they want.'

'They're leaving sub-space and gaining altitude.' Cal interjected. 'They are in space...losing their signal.'

'They're leaving even without a *thank you*.' Professor Hogan replied. 'Amazing...'

'Object is now on the TV screens, Dudes.' Jergel said. 'Look out people.'

'Getting a good view on the scope.' Breyer said. 'Size is decent...heard of bigger.'

'Yeah, it's big enough though, Bob.' The Professor said peering through the scope. 'Let's hang tight.'

Olivia scanned her screens with intensity. 'The trajectory has it hitting at the center of the Atlantic Ocean.'

Jess groaned. 'That would cause enormous tidal waves on all sides of the Atlantic. I don't want to watch this.'

'People are going crazy!' Jergel yelled. 'Look at these scenes in New York and the east coast...Europe...Africa...Central America...South America! Heck, I'm locking the doors on this truck.'

'Definitely in view now,' Breyer said as he looked over at the professor. The professor confirmed his sighting also.

'Okay, let's just track it and see what happens...nothing more we can do, unfortunately.' The Professor replied returning to his scope. 'As soon as it hits, everyone can head home and take care of things...if the roads aren't entirely congested with the panic stricken.'

The crew quietly monitored the situation with concern. They were the astronomers. They were the experts in this field, yet they felt so helpless. In the background, the news reports blared with pending disaster and the projection of unknown consequences, which only added to their feeling of helplessness. Somehow, they felt as though they were letting everyone down.

'The asteroid is shifting...very odd.' Cal spewed to the group. 'It is no longer on a direct trajectory to the original location. It would be several miles away with this movement.'

'It shifted??' Breyer asked excitedly. 'Can't be!'

'Yes, my screens show a deviation of the approach…it's even increasing.' Jess replied.

'Confirmed,' Cal retorted. 'Deviation is increasing…it's gaining altitude.'

'Let's keep an eye on it, folks, this is odd.' The Professor said. 'What are they saying on the news reports, Jergel?'

'No news, Professor, they may not be able to tell unless the observatories report it.' He answered.

'Logical. What does the radar show now, Cal?' He said.

Cal looked intensely at his screen. 'Same sequence of altitude adjustments…continued slight pattern and increasing. This is extremely odd, but…a good thing if it continues.'

'At this pace it will leave the atmosphere…unbelievable!' Breyer said with excitement.

'I can see it with the naked eye.' The Professor replied. 'I can see it moving higher in altitude…it's getting smaller in the scope's visual.'

'Confirming all of your analyses…it is moving into sub-space!' Jess blurted. 'Unheard of!'

'Keep going…just keep going!' Jergel said.

'If I'm right…it will be back into space within minutes…and I'm hoping I'm right!' Cal said with a smile. 'Hey! Two objects now appearing on the radar in the vicinity!'

'Two? Watcha got, big boy?' Jess said without removing her gaze from the screens.

'It's the craft! It's back…and near the asteroid!' Cal answered in amazement.

'The craft is back?' Jess replied.

'No doubt…it's the craft. Nothing else could be up there and it is within a short distance to the approaching object.' Cal answered.

'Oh, man! What is going on??' Jergel said throwing himself into his chair.

'The object is still gaining altitude…' Olivia replied.

'It's heading away, my friends. It's heading away from our blue planet.' Breyer said in a soft and eloquent tone.

'I would agree, Bob. It does appear so.' The Professor slowly replied while staring through his telescope. 'But, how is it possible? Everything in science and astronomy would say that this is unheard of.'

Cal sighed. 'Let's make one thing clear, my friends…there is no coincidence that *they* were near the asteroid…and it now is moving past us. Let's make that very clear. Professor Hogan…I believe that they just said…*thank you.*'

CHAPTER 17

On April 22, 2015, former Canadian Defense Minister, Paul Hellyer, stated during a speech at the University of Calgary that aliens have been visiting Earth for thousands of years – four species in particular. He noted that many walk among us, but are difficult to distinguish between humans. He also mentioned that other species are more "creature-like." Hellyer stated that governments are aware of 12 alien species and, possibly, as many as 80.

He continued by stating that most aliens are benevolent and have far-advanced and vastly superior technology. They have only assisted governments to a small degree, since they are disappointed in our ways of living. They have stated that Earthlings spend too much time on war and military efforts and not enough on the sick, homeless and poor. They proclaim that they will pass on their technology when they see a change in our way of life.

With the asteroid completely missing an earthly impact the astronomy and science worlds were in a self-imposed state of shock. Astronomers stumbled over their words in interviews on national broadcasts. They had no explanation for the event, but were very pleased that the impact did not occur. They could only say that the movement of the asteroid – away from the projected impact – was as surprising as its appearance in the first place.

Cal and the university team were glued to the television in the mobile observatory unit. They watched the broadcasts and feeds from their colleagues around the world. Cal walked outside and leaned against the truck. Soon, the others followed.

'I would love to explain to the media what occurred.' He said. 'But, I dare not. I don't think that it's the right time, plus…we have no way of proving it.'

Jess slowly walked up to him and gently nestled up against his chest. She looked up and kissed him softly on the cheek. 'It's our secret, big boy… at least for now.'

He looked at her, smiled and pulled her closer. 'You're right…girlfriend.' Professor Hogan cleared his throat. 'I believe that it's the prudent approach at this time. Are we all in agreement?'

The group nodded simultaneously.

Their minute of contemplating silence was broken by an audible tone emanating from inside the mobile unit. It was clearly the radar system and Cal and Jess looked at each other and then immediately climbed into the truck. Cal sat down at the workstation with Jess peering over his shoulder.

'They're back! The craft is back!' Cal exclaimed.

Jess rubbed his shoulders. 'Sure looks that way...but, why? They should have what they need.'

The others peaked into the door and Jess explained that the visitors had returned. The computer screens soon blinked and then went completely blank. An audible tone then came across the speakers. Once again, a digital message appeared across the screens. The crew climbed back into the truck and began to capture the message, which was lengthier than those previously received. Olivia and Breyer began to feed the message through the translation software and, several minutes later, the coding was broken.

'Here it is.' Olivia said pulling up the information on a laptop. 'Loosely translated, of course.'

One visited your third planet from your star... Earth... years past...for resources not in our galactic realm...two planet coordinates provided our needs.

(Coordinates for Peru and Hy Brasil appeared)

The first coordinate was exhausted on One's second visit to the third planet... Earth years later....Much time has past and One's needs arose again...A beacon was jettisoned to discover the location still plentiful of resources on the third planet...One's beacon was lost...an earth probe (a small graphic of the Pioneer probe) *led us to the third planet...your human species assistance requires gratitude.*

One has visited the third planet twice before...we have watched your evolution...One is disappointed...third planet species continues to...conduct inter-species battles...and inappropriate acts against each other...on One's last visit...we intervened to halt continued battles... (graphic of Alexander's battle in India appears)*...yet they continue to this Earth day...One hopes* *for your species tranquility…to evolve…One issues gratitude for your assistance…One hopes that gratitude has been returned. We will provide you with additional gratitude… to cure many of your species ills…when further evolution is proven.*

The crew, viewing the screens, was totally speechless. Jess turned to the radar and proclaimed that they were gone.

Cal stood up and ran his hand through his hair. 'We've experienced something incredible here tonight.' He said. 'They're right, you know… humans are still very primitive. Watch the evening news if you want proof.'

Professor Hogan nodded strongly. 'Yes…we need to really look at ourselves. We really do. This proves that we are not the center of the universe…and we have a long, long way to go to ever become that.'

'I have to give you credit, Cal. Your NASA training must have been very good…you deciphered their purpose here almost exactly.' Breyer interjected.

Cal smiled. 'Thanks. I study history, archaeology and astronomy more than I probably should. They are often tied together…as we've seen here.'

'What were they talking about when they mentioned Alexander?' Jess asked.

'Alexander the Great…the Greek general that was basically conquering the world.' Cal replied. 'His military was unstoppable and they had rolled through the Middle East and were heading towards India in 329 BC. They were in the process of invading India when…per some historical records…they were attacked by objects in the sky.' Cal paused to study their amazed faces. 'Alexander's army was rattled and refused to continue…they eventually returned home and their conquests were halted.'

'So, our visitors…"*One*"…claims that it was they who stopped the conquests.' Professor Hogan interjected. 'I have heard of the incident… this is amazing.'

'Yes,' Cal said. 'They halted an…*inter-species battle.*'

Needing some air, Cal slowly walked out of the rear door of the mobile observatory with Jess following. He leaned against the truck and looked up into the clear, star-filled sky. It seemed different tonight. The night sky spoke to him…literally. The astronomy world was king tonight and he couldn't be more pleased. Jess softly sang a tune as he held her. It was a classic Frank Sinatra melody.

Fly me to the moon
Let me play among the stars
Let me see what spring is like on a Jupiter and Mars
In other words, hold my hand
In other words, baby, kiss me…

And Cal did both. Her voice was beautiful tonight and that made him believe that everything in the world could be better.

ALLEGHENY OBSERVATORY

Tribute to the Allegheny Observatory, which stoked my interest in astronomy-

Per Wikipedia:

The Allegheny Observatory is a major astronomical research institution, located in Riverview Park in Pittsburgh, and is part of the Department of Physics and Astronomy at the University of Pittsburgh. The main active research pursuit at the Allegheny Observatory involves detections of extrasolar planets. This is done using photometry, which is the practice of measuring the brightness of stars. The brightness of a target star and its close neighbors are measured on digital images taken every 30–60 seconds, and if a planet crosses (transits) in front of its parent star's disk, then the observed visual brightness of the star drops a small amount. The amount the star dims depends on the relative sizes of the star and the planet. The observatory operates three large telescopes: Thaw Refractor, Keeler Reflector and Fitz-Clark Refractor.

Famous astronomers have been associated with the observatory: John Brashear, S.P. Langley and James Keeler

The history of the Allegheny Observatory was put to film in - *Undaunted – The the Fogotten Giants of the Allegheny Observatory*. Commentary by Neil deGrasse Tyson and narrated by David Conrad. Available for purchase through Amazon.com and other online retailers. The observatory also offers public tours.

The facility is listed on the National Register of Historical Places and is designated as a Pennsylvania state and Pittsburgh History and Landmarks Foundation historic landmark. The original observatory was opened in 1859.

Bibliography:

- *Popular Science Magazine*
- *NOVA – PBS*
- *Ancient Aliens – History Channel*
- *Pittsburgh Post-Gazette – News Articles*
- *Wikipedia*
- *Various Internet Websites*

Printed in the United States
By Bookmasters